A Beleaguered City

Mrs. Oliphant

DODO
PRESS

A BELEAGUERED CITY

BEING

A NARRATIVE OF CERTAIN RECENT EVENTS IN THE CITY OF SEMUR, IN THE DEPARTMENT OF THE HAUTE BOURGOGNE

A STORY OF THE SEEN AND THE UNSEEN

by Mrs. Oliphant

1900

THE AUTHOR inscribes this little Book, with tender and grateful greetings, to those whose sympathy has supported her through many and long years, the kind audience of her UNKNOWN FRIENDS.

THE NARRATIVE OF M. LE MAIRE: THE CONDITION OF THE CITY.

I, Martin Dupin (de la Clairière), had the honour of holding the office of Maire in the town of Semur, in the Haute Bourgogne, at the time when the following events occurred. It will be perceived, therefore, that no one could have more complete knowledge of the facts—at once from my official position, and from the place of eminence in the affairs of the district generally which my family has held for many generations—by what citizen-like virtues and unblemished integrity I will not be vain enough to specify. Nor is it necessary; for no one who knows Semur can be ignorant of the position held by the Dupins, from father to son. The estate La Clairière has been so long in the family that we might very well, were we disposed, add its name to our own, as so many families in France do; and, indeed, I do not prevent my wife (whose prejudices I respect) from making this use of it upon her cards. But, for myself, *bourgeois* I was born and *bourgeois* I mean to die. My residence, like that of my father and grandfather, is at No. 29 in the Grande Rue, opposite the Cathedral, and not far from the Hospital of St. Jean. We inhabit the first floor, along with the *rez-de-chaussée,* which has been turned into domestic offices suitable for the needs of the family. My mother, holding a respected place in my household, lives with us in the most perfect family union. My wife (*née* de Champfleurie) is everything that is calculated to render a household happy; but, alas one only of our two children survives to bless us. I have thought these details of my private circumstances necessary, to explain the following narrative; to which I will also add, by way of introduction, a simple sketch of the town itself and its general conditions before these remarkable events occurred.

It was on a summer evening about sunset, the middle of the month of June, that my attention was attracted by an incident of no importance which occurred in the street, when I was making my way home, after an inspection of the young vines in my new vineyard to the left of La Clairière. All were in perfectly good condition, and none of the many signs which point to the arrival of the insect were apparent. I had come back in good spirits, thinking of the prosperity which I was happy to believe I had merited by a conscientious performance of all my duties. I had little with which to blame myself: not only my wife and relations, but my dependants and neighbours, approved my conduct as a man; and even my fellow-citizens, exacting as they are, had confirmed in my favour the good opinion which my family had been fortunate enough to secure from father to son. These thoughts were in my mind as I turned the corner of the Grande Rue and approached my own house. At this moment the tinkle of a little bell warned all the bystanders of the procession which was about to pass, carrying the rites of the Church to some dying person. Some of the women, always devout, fell on their knees. I did not go so far as this, for I do not pretend, in these days of progress, to have retained the same attitude of mind as that which it is no doubt becoming to behold in the more devout sex; but I stood respectfully out of the way, and took off my hat, as good breeding alone, if nothing else, demanded of me. Just in front of me, however, was Jacques Richard, always a troublesome individual, standing doggedly, with his hat upon his head and his hands in his pockets, straight in the path of M. le Curé. There is not in all France a more obstinate fellow. He stood there, notwithstanding the efforts of a good woman to draw him away, and though I myself called to him. M. le Curé is not the man to flinch; and as he passed, walking as usual very quickly and straight, his soutane brushed against the blouse of Jacques. He gave one quick glance from beneath his eyebrows at the profane interruption, but he would not distract himself from his sacred errand at such a moment. It is a sacred errand when any one, be he priest or layman, carries the best he can give to the bedside of the dying. I said this to Jacques when M. le Curé had passed and the bell went tinkling on along the street. 'Jacques, ' said I, 'I do not call it impious, like this good woman, but I call it inhuman. What! a man goes to carry help to the dying, and you show him no respect! '

This brought the colour to his face; and I think, perhaps, that he might have become ashamed of the part he had played; but the women pushed in again, as they are so fond of doing. 'Oh, M. le Maire, he does not deserve that you should lose your words upon him! ' they cried; 'and, besides, is it likely he will pay any attention to you when he tries to stop even the *bon Dieu*? '

'The *bon Dieu! '* cried Jacques. 'Why doesn't He clear the way for himself? Look here. I do not care one farthing for your *bon Dieu*. Here is mine; I carry him about with me. ' And he took a piece of a hundred sous out of his pocket (how had it got there?) *'Vive l'argent'* he said. 'You know it yourself, though you will not say so. There is no *bon Dieu* but money. With money you can do anything. *L'argent c'est le bon Dieu.* '

'Be silent, ' I cried, 'thou profane one! ' And the women were still more indignant than I. 'We shall see, we shall see; when he is ill and would give his soul for something to wet his lips, his *bon Dieu* will not do much for him, ' cried one; and another said, clasping her hands with a shrill cry, 'It is enough to make the dead rise out of their graves! '

'The dead rise out of their graves! ' These words, though one has heard them before, took possession of my imagination. I saw the rude fellow go along the street as I went on, tossing the coin in his hand. One time it fell to the ground and rang upon the pavement, and he laughed more loudly as he picked it up. He was walking towards the sunset, and I too, at a distance after. The sky was full of rose-tinted clouds floating across the blue, floating high over the grey pinnacles of the Cathedral, and filling the long open line of the Rue St. Etienne down which he was going. As I crossed to my own house I caught him full against the light, in his blue blouse, tossing the big silver piece in the air, and heard him laugh and shout *'Vive l'argent!* This is the only *bon Dieu.* ' Though there are many people who live as if this were their sentiment, there are few who give it such brutal expression; but some of the people at the corner of the street laughed too. 'Bravo, Jacques! ' they cried; and one said, 'You are right, *mon ami,* the only god to trust in nowadays. ' 'It is a short *credo,* M. le Maire, ' said another, who caught my eye. He saw I was displeased, this one, and his countenance changed at once.

'Yes, Jean Pierre, ' I said, 'it is worse than short—it is brutal. I hope no man who respects himself will ever countenance it. It is against the dignity of human nature, if nothing more. '

'Ah, M. le Maire! ' cried a poor woman, one of the good ladies of the market, with entrenchments of baskets all round her, who had been walking my way; 'ah, M. le Maire! did not I say true? it is enough to bring the dead out of their graves. '

'That would be something to see, ' said Jean Pierre, with a laugh; 'and I hope, *ma bonne femme,* that if you have any interest with them, you will entreat these gentlemen to appear before I go away. '

'I do not like such jesting, ' said I. 'The dead are very dead and will not disturb anybody, but even the prejudices of respectable persons ought to be respected. A ribald like Jacques counts for nothing, but I did not expect this from you. '

'What would you, M. le Maire? ' he said, with a shrug of his shoulders. 'We are made like that. I respect prejudices as you say. My wife is a good woman, she prays for two—but me! How can I tell that Jacques is not right after all? A *grosse pièce* of a hundred sous, one sees that, one knows what it can do—but for the other! ' He thrust up one shoulder to his ear, and turned up the palms of his hands.

'It is our duty at all times to respect the convictions of others, ' I said, severely; and passed on to my own house, having no desire to encourage discussions at the street corner. A man in my position is obliged to be always mindful of the example he ought to set. But I had not yet done with this phrase, which had, as I have said, caught my ear and my imagination. My mother was in the great *salle* of the *rez-de-chausée,* as I passed, in altercation with a peasant who had just brought us in some loads of wood. There is often, it seems to me, a sort of *refrain* in conversation, which one catches everywhere as one comes and goes. Figure my astonishment when I heard from the lips of my good mother the same words with which that good-for-nothing Jacques Richard had made the profession of his brutal faith. 'Go! ' she cried, in anger; 'you are all the same. Money is your god. *De grosses pièces,* that is all you think of in these days. '

'*Eh, bien,* madame, ' said the peasant; 'and if so, what then? Don't you others, gentlemen and ladies, do just the same? What is there in the world but money to think of? If it is a question of marriage, you demand what is the *dot*; if it is a question of office, you ask, Monsieur Untel, is he rich? And it is perfectly just. We know what money can do; but as for *le bon Dieu,* whom our grandmothers used to talk about—'

And lo! our *gros paysan* made exactly the same gesture as Jean Pierre. He put up his shoulders to his ears, and spread out the palms of his hands, as who should say, There is nothing further to be said.

Then there occurred a still more remarkable repetition. My mother, as may be supposed, being a very respectable person, and more or less *dévote,* grew red with indignation and horror.

'Oh, these poor grandmothers! ' she cried; 'God give them rest! It is enough to make the dead rise out of their graves. '

'Oh, I will answer for *les morts*! they will give nobody any trouble, ' he said with a laugh. I went in and reproved the man severely, finding that, as I supposed, he had attempted to cheat my good mother in the price of the wood. Fortunately she had been quite as clever as he was. She went upstairs shaking her head, while I gave the man to understand that no one should speak to her but with the profoundest respect in my house. 'She has her opinions, like all respectable ladies, ' I said, 'but under this roof these opinions shall always be sacred. ' And, to do him justice, I will add that when it was put to him in this way Gros-Jean was ashamed of himself.

When I talked over these incidents with my wife, as we gave each other the narrative of our day's experiences, she was greatly distressed, as may be supposed. 'I try to hope they are not so bad as Bonne Maman thinks. But oh, *mon ami!* ' she said, 'what will the world come to if this is what they really believe? '

'Take courage, ' I said; 'the world will never come to anything much different from what it is. So long as there are *des anges* like thee to pray for us, the scale will not go down to the wrong side. '

I said this, of course, to please my Agnès, who is the best of wives; but on thinking it over after, I could not but be struck with the extreme justice (not to speak of the beauty of the sentiment) of this thought. The *bon Dieu*—if, indeed, that great Being is as represented to us by the Church—must naturally care as much for one-half of His creatures as for the other, though they have not the same weight in the world; and consequently the faith of the women must hold the balance straight, especially if, as is said, they exceed us in point of numbers. This leaves a little margin for those of them who profess the same freedom of thought as is generally accorded to men—a class, I must add, which I abominate from the bottom of my heart.

I need not dwell upon other little scenes which impressed the same idea still more upon my mind. Semur, I need not say, is not the centre of the world, and might, therefore, be supposed likely to escape the full current of worldliness. We amuse ourselves little, and we have not any opportunity of rising to the heights of ambition; for our town is not even the *chef-lieu* of the department, —though this is a subject upon which I cannot trust myself to speak. Figure to yourself that La Rochette—a place of yesterday, without either the beauty or the antiquity of Semur—has been chosen as the centre of affairs, the residence of M. le Préfet! But I will not enter upon this question. What I was saying was, that, notwithstanding the fact that we amuse ourselves but little, that there is no theatre to speak of, little society, few distractions, and none of those inducements to strive for gain and to indulge the senses, which exist, for instance, in Paris—that capital of the world—yet, nevertheless, the thirst for money and for pleasure has increased among us to an extent which I cannot but consider alarming. Gros-Jean, our peasant, toils for money, and hoards; Jacques, who is a cooper and maker of wine casks, gains and drinks; Jean Pierre snatches at every sous that comes in his way, and spends it in yet worse dissipations. He is one who quails when he meets my eye; he sins *en cachette*; but Jacques is bold, and defies opinion; and Gros-Jean is firm in the belief that to hoard money is the highest of mortal occupations. These three are types of what the population is at Semur. The men would all sell their souls for a *grosse pièce* of fifty sous—indeed, they would laugh, and express their delight that any one should believe them to love souls, if they could but have a chance of selling them; and the devil, who was once supposed to deal in that commodity, would be very welcome among us. And as for the *bon Dieu—pouff!* that was an affair of the grandmothers—*le bon Dieu c'est l'argent*. This is their creed. I was very near the beginning of my official year as Maire when my attention was called to these matters as I have described above. A man may go on for years keeping quiet himself—keeping out of tumult, religious or political—and make no discovery of the general current of feeling; but when you are forced to serve your country in any official capacity, and when your eyes are opened to the state of affairs around you, then I allow that an inexperienced observer might well cry out, as my wife did, 'What will become of the world? ' I am not prejudiced myself—unnecessary to say that the foolish scruples of the women do not move me. But the devotion of the community at large to this pursuit of gain-money without any grandeur, and pleasure without any refinement—that is a thing which cannot fail to wound all who believe in human nature. To be a millionaire—that, I grant, would be pleasant. A man as rich as Monte Christo, able to do whatever he would, with the equipage of an English duke, the palace of an Italian prince, the retinue of a Russian noble—he, indeed, might be excused if his money seemed to him a kind of god. But Gros-Jean, who lays up two sous at a time, and lives on black bread and an onion; and Jacques, whose *grosse pièce* but secures him the headache of a drunkard next morning—what to them could be this miserable deity? As for myself, however, it was my business, as Maire of the commune, to take as little notice as possible of the follies these people might say, and to hold the middle course between the prejudices of the respectable and the levities of the foolish. With this, without more, to think of, I had enough to keep all my faculties employed.

THE NARRATIVE OF M. LE MAIRE CONTINUED: BEGINNING OF THE LATE REMARKABLE EVENTS.

I do not attempt to make out any distinct connection between the simple incidents above recorded, and the extraordinary events that followed. I have related them as they happened; chiefly by way of showing the state of feeling in the city, and the sentiment which pervaded the community—a sentiment, I fear, too common in my country. I need not say that to encourage superstition is far from my wish. I am a man of my century, and proud of being so; very little disposed to yield to the domination of the clerical party, though desirous of showing all just tolerance for conscientious faith, and every respect for the prejudices of the ladies of my family. I am, moreover, all the more inclined to be careful of giving in my adhesion to any prodigy, in consequence of a consciousness that the faculty of imagination has always been one of my characteristics. It usually is so, I am aware, in superior minds, and it has procured me many pleasures unknown to the common herd. Had it been possible for me to believe that I had been misled by this faculty, I should have carefully refrained from putting upon record any account of my individual impressions; but my attitude here is not that of a man recording his personal experiences only, but of one who is the official mouthpiece and representative of the commune, and whose duty it is to render to government and to the human race a true narrative of the very wonderful facts to which every citizen of Semur can bear witness. In this capacity it has become my duty so to arrange and edit the different accounts of the mystery, as to present one coherent and trustworthy chronicle to the world.

To proceed, however, with my narrative. It is not necessary for me to describe what summer is in the Haute Bourgogne. Our generous wines, our glorious fruits, are sufficient proof, without any assertion on my part. The summer with us is as a perpetual *fête*—at least, before the insect appeared it was so, though now anxiety about the condition of our vines may cloud our enjoyment of the glorious sunshine which ripens them hourly before our eyes. Judge, then, of the astonishment of the world when there suddenly came upon us a darkness as in the depth of winter, falling, without warning, into the midst of the brilliant weather to which we are accustomed, and which had never failed us before in the memory of man! It was the month of July, when, in ordinary seasons, a cloud is so rare that it is a joy to see one, merely as a variety upon the brightness. Suddenly, in the midst of our summer delights, this darkness came. Its first appearance took us so entirely by surprise that life seemed to stop short, and the business of the whole town was delayed by an hour or two; nobody being able to believe that at six o'clock in the morning the sun had not risen. I do not assert that the sun did not rise; all I mean to say is that at Semur it was still dark, as in a morning of winter, and when it gradually and slowly became day many hours of the morning were already spent. And never shall I forget the aspect of day when it came. It was like a ghost or pale shadow of the glorious days of July with which we are usually blessed. The barometer did not go down, nor was there any rain, but an unusual greyness wrapped earth and sky. I heard people say in the streets, and I am aware that the same words came to my own lips: 'If it were not full summer, I should say it was going to snow. ' We have much snow in the Haute Bourgogne, and we are well acquainted with this aspect of the skies. Of the depressing effect which this greyness exercised upon myself personally, greyness exercised upon myself personally, I will not speak. I have always been noted as a man of fine perceptions, and I was aware instinctively that such a state of the atmosphere must mean something more than was apparent on the surface. But, as the danger was of an entirely unprecedented character, it is not to be wondered at that I should be completely at a loss to divine what its meaning was. It was a blight some people said; and many were of opinion that it was caused by clouds of animalculæ coming, as is described in ancient writings, to destroy the crops, and even to affect the health of the population. The doctors scoffed at this; but they talked about malaria, which, as far as I could understand, was likely to produce exactly the same effect. The night closed in early as the day had dawned late; the lamps were lighted before six o'clock, and daylight had only begun about ten! Figure to yourself, a July day! There ought to have been a moon almost at the full; but no moon was visible, no stars—nothing but a grey veil of clouds, growing darker and darker as the moments went on; such I have heard are the days and the nights in England, where the seafogs so often blot out the sky. But we are unacquainted with anything of the kind in our *plaisant pays de France*. There was nothing else talked of in Semur all that night, as may well be imagined. My own mind was extremely uneasy. Do what I would, I could not deliver myself from a sense of something dreadful in the air which was neither malaria nor animalculæ, I took a promenade through the streets that evening, accompanied by M. Barbou, my *adjoint*, to make sure that all was safe; and the darkness was such that we almost lost our way, though we were both born in the town and had known every turning from our boyhood. It cannot be denied that Semur is very badly lighted. We retain still the lanterns slung by cords across the streets which once were general in France, but which, in most places, have been superseded by the modern institution of gas. Gladly would I have distinguished my term of office by bringing gas to Semur. But the expense would have been great, and there were a hundred objections. In summer generally, the lanterns were of little consequence because of the brightness of the sky; but to see them now, twinkling dimly here and there, making us conscious how dark it was, was strange indeed. It was in the interests of order that we took our round, with a fear, in my mind at least, of I knew not what. M. l'Adjoint said nothing, but no doubt he thought as I did.

While we were thus patrolling the city with a special eye to the prevention of all seditious assemblages, such as are too apt to take advantage of any circumstances that may disturb the ordinary life of a city, or throw discredit on its magistrates, we were accosted by Paul Lecamus, a man whom I have always considered as something of a visionary, though his conduct is irreproachable, and his life honourable and industrious. He entertains religious convictions of a curious kind; but, as the man is quite free from revolutionary sentiments, I have never considered it to be my duty to interfere with him, or to investigate his creed. Indeed, he has been treated generally in Semur as a dreamer of dreams—one who holds a great many impracticable and foolish opinions—though the respect which I always exact for those whose lives are respectable and worthy has been a protection to hire. He was, I think, aware that he owed something to my good offices, and it was to me accordingly that he addressed himself.

'Good evening, M. le Maire, ' he said; 'you are groping about, like myself, in this strange night. '

'Good evening M. Paul, ' I replied. 'It is, indeed, a strange night. It indicates, I fear, that a storm is coming. '

M. Paul shook his head. There is a solemnity about even his ordinary appearance. He has a long face, pale, and adorned with a heavy, drooping moustache, which adds much to the solemn impression made by his countenance. He looked at me with great gravity as he stood in the shadow of the lamp, and slowly shook his head.

'You do not agree with me? Well! the opinion of a man like M. Paul Lecamus is always worthy to be heard.'

'Oh!' he said, 'I am called visionary. I am not supposed to be a trustworthy witness. Nevertheless, if M. Le Maire will come with me, I will show him something that is very strange—something that is almost more wonderful than the darkness—more strange,' he went on with great earnestness, 'than any storm that ever ravaged Burgundy.'

'That is much to say. A tempest now when the vines are in full bearing—'

'Would be nothing, nothing to what I can show you. Only come with me to the Porte St. Lambert.'

'If M. le Maire will excuse me,' said M. Barbou, 'I think I will go home. It is a little cold, and you are aware that I am always afraid of the damp.' In fact, our coats were beaded with a cold dew as in November, and I could not but acknowledge that my respectable colleague had reason. Besides, we were close to his house, and he had, no doubt, the sustaining consciousness of having done everything that was really incumbent upon him. 'Our ways lie together as far as my house,' he said, with a slight chattering of his teeth. No doubt it was the cold. After we had walked with him to his door, we proceeded to the Porte St. Lambert. By this time almost everybody had re-entered their houses. The streets were very dark, and they were also very still. When we reached the gates, at that hour of the night, we found them shut as a matter of course. The officers of the *octroi* were standing close together at the door of their office, in which the lamp was burning. The very lamp seemed oppressed by the heavy air; it burnt dully, surrounded with a yellow haze. The men had the appearance of suffering greatly from cold. They received me with a satisfaction which was very gratifying to me. 'At length here is M. le Maire himself,' they said.

'My good friends,' said I, 'you have a cold post to-night. The weather has changed in the most extraordinary way. I have no doubt the scientific gentlemen at the Musée will be able to tell us all about it—M. de Clairon—'

'Not to interrupt M. le Maire,' said Riou, of the *octroi*, 'I think there is more in it than any scientific gentleman can explain.'

'Ah! You think so. But they explain everything, ' I said, with a smile. 'They tell us how the wind is going to blow. '

As I said this, there seemed to pass us, from the direction of the closed gates, a breath of air so cold that I could not restrain a shiver. They looked at each other. It was not a smile that passed between them—they were too pale, too cold, to smile but a look of intelligence. 'M. le Maire, ' said one of them, 'perceives it too; ' but they did not shiver as I did. They were like men turned into ice who could feel no more.

'It is, without doubt, the most extraordinary weather, ' I said. My teeth chattered like Barbou's. It was all I could do to keep myself steady. No one made any reply; but Lecamus said, 'Have the goodness to open the little postern for foot-passengers: M. le Maire wishes to make an inspection outside. '

Upon these words, Riou, who knew me well, caught me by the arm. 'A thousand pardons, ' he said, 'M. le Maire; but I entreat you, do not go. Who can tell what is outside? Since this morning there is something very strange on the other side of the gates. If M. le Maire would listen to me, he would keep them shut night and day till *that* is gone, he would not go out into the midst of it. *Mon Dieu!* a man may be brave. I know the courage of M. le Maire; but to march without necessity into the jaws of hell: *mon Dieu!* ' cried the poor man again. He crossed himself, and none of us smiled. Now a man may sign himself at the church door—one does so out of respect; but to use that ceremony for one's own advantage, before other men, is rare—except in the case of members of a very decided party. Riou was not one of these. He signed himself in sight of us all, and not one of us smiled.

The other was less familiar—he knew me only in my public capacity—he was one Gallais of the Quartier St. Médon. He said, taking off his hat: 'If I were M. le Maire, saving your respect, I would not go out into an unknown danger with this man here, a man who is known as a pietist, as a clerical, as one who sees visions—'

'He is not a clerical, he is a good citizen, ' I said; 'come, lend us your lantern. Shall I shrink from my duty wherever it leads me? Nay, my good friends, the Maire of a French commune fears neither man nor devil in the exercise of his duty. M. Paul, lead on. ' When I said the word 'devil' a spasm of alarm passed over Riou's face. He crossed himself again. This time I could not but smile. 'My little Riou, ' I said, 'do you know that you are a little imbecile with your piety? There is a time for everything. '

'Except religion, M. le Maire; that is never out of place, ' said Gallais.

I could not believe my senses. 'Is it a conversion? ' I said. 'Some of our Carmes déchaussés must have passed this way. '

'M. le Maire will soon see other teachers more wonderful than the Carmes déchaussés, ' said Lecamus. He went and took down the lantern from its nail, and opened the little door. When it opened, I was once more penetrated by the same icy breath; once, twice, thrice, I cannot tell how many times this crossed me, as if some one passed. I looked round upon the others—I gave way a step. I could not help it. In spite of me, the hair seemed to rise erect on my head. The two officers stood close together, and Riou, collecting his courage, made an attempt to laugh. 'M. le Maire perceives, ' he said, his lips trembling almost too much to form the words, 'that the winds are walking about. ' 'Hush, for God's sake! ' said the other, grasping him by the arm.

This recalled me to myself; and I followed Lecamus, who stood waiting for me holding the door a little ajar. He went on strangely, like—I can use no other words to express it—a man making his way in the face of a crowd, a thing very surprising to me. I followed him close; but the moment I emerged from the doorway something caught my breath. The same feeling seized me also. I gasped; a sense of suffocation came upon me; I put out my hand to lay hold upon my guide. The solid grasp I got of his arm re-assured me a little, and he did not hesitate, but pushed his way on. We got out clear of the gate and the shadow of the wall, keeping close to the little watch-tower on the west side. Then he made a pause, and so did I. We stood against the tower and looked out before us. There was nothing there. The darkness was great, yet through the gloom of the night I could see the division of the road from the broken ground on either side; there was nothing there. I gasped, and drew myself up close against the wall, as Lecamus had also done. There was in the air, in the night, a sensation the most strange I have ever experienced. I have felt the same thing indeed at other times, in face of a great crowd, when thousands of people were moving, rustling, struggling, breathing around me, thronging all the vacant space, filling up every spot. This was the sensation that overwhelmed me here—a crowd:

yet nothing to be seen but the darkness, the indistinct line of the road. We could not move for them, so close were they round us. What do I say? There was nobody—nothing—not a form to be seen, not a face but his and mine. I am obliged to confess that the moment was to me an awful moment. I could not speak. My heart beat wildly as if trying to escape from my breast—every breath I drew was with an effort. I clung to Lecamus with deadly and helpless terror, and forced myself back upon the wall, crouching against it; I did not turn and fly, as would have been natural. What say I? *did* not! I *could* not! they pressed round us so. Ah! you would think I must be mad to use such words, for there was nobody near me—not a shadow even upon the road.

Lecamus would have gone farther on; he would have pressed his way boldly into the midst; but my courage was not equal to this. I clutched and clung to him, dragging myself along against the wall, my whole mind intent upon getting back. I was stronger than he, and he had no power to resist me. I turned back, stumbling blindly, keeping my face to that crowd (there was no one), but struggling back again, tearing the skin off my hands as I groped my way along the wall. Oh, the agony of seeing the door closed! I have buffeted my way through a crowd before now, but I may say that I never before knew what terror was. When I fell upon the door, dragging Lecamus with me, it opened, thank God! I stumbled in, clutching at Riou with my disengaged hand, and fell upon the floor of the *octroi*, where they thought I had fainted. But this was not the case. A man of resolution may give way to the overpowering sensations of the moment. His bodily faculties may fail him; but his mind will not fail. As in every really superior intelligence, my forces collected for the emergency. While the officers ran to bring me water, to search for the eau-de vie which they had in a cupboard, I astonished them all by rising up, pale, but with full command of myself. 'It is enough, ' I said, raising my hand. 'I thank you, Messieurs, but nothing more is necessary; ' and I would not take any of their restoratives. They were impressed, as was only natural, by the sight of my perfect self-possession: it helped them to acquire for themselves a demeanour befitting the occasion; and I felt, though still in great physical weakness and agitation, the consoling consciousness of having fulfilled my functions as head of the community.

'M. le Maire has seen a——what there is outside? ' Riou cried, stammering in his excitement; and the other fixed upon me eyes which were hungering with eagerness—if, indeed, it is permitted to use such words.

'I have seen—nothing, Riou, ' I said.

They looked at me with the utmost wonder. 'M. le Maire has seen—nothing? ' said Riou. 'Ah, I see! you say so to spare us. We have proved ourselves cowards; but if you will pardon me, M. le Maire, you, too, re-entered precipitately—you too! There are facts which may appal the bravest—but I implore you to tell us what you have seen. '

'I have seen nothing, ' I said. As I spoke, my natural calm composure returned, my heart resumed its usual tranquil beating. 'There is nothing to be seen—it is dark, and one can perceive the line of the road for but a little way—that is all. There is nothing to be seen——'

They looked at me, startled and incredulous. They did not know what to think. How could they refuse to believe me, sitting there calmly raising my eyes to them, making my statement with what they felt to be an air of perfect truth? But, then, how account for the precipitate return which they had already noted, the supposed faint, the pallor of my looks? They did not know what to think.

And here, let me remark, as in my conduct throughout these remarkable events, may be seen the benefit, the high advantage, of truth. Had not this been the truth, I could not have borne the searching of their looks. But it was true. There was nothing—nothing to be seen; in one sense, this was the thing of all others which overwhelmed my mind. But why insist upon these matters of detail to unenlightened men? There was nothing, and I had seen nothing. What I said was the truth.

All this time Lecamus had said nothing. As I raised myself from the ground, I had vaguely perceived him hanging up the lantern where it had been before; now he became distinct to me as I recovered the full possession of my faculties. He had seated himself upon a bench by the wall. There was no agitation about him; no sign of the thrill of departing excitement, which I felt going through my veins as through the strings of a harp. He was sitting against the wall, with his head drooping, his eyes cast down, an air of disappointment and despondency about him—nothing more. I got up as soon as I felt that I could go away with perfect propriety; but, before I left the place, called him. He got up when he heard his name, but he did it with reluctance. He came with me because I asked him to do so, not from any wish of his own. Very different were the feelings of Riou and Gallais. They did their utmost to engage me in conversation, to consult me about a hundred trifles, to ask me with the greatest deference what they ought to do in such and such cases, pressing close to me, trying every expedient to delay my departure. When we went away they stood at the door of their little office close together, looking after us with looks which I found it difficult to forget; they would not abandon their post; but their faces were pale and contracted, their eyes wild with anxiety and distress.

It was only as I walked away, hearing my own steps and those of Lecamus ringing upon the pavement, that I began to realise what had happened. The effort of recovering my composure, the relief from the extreme excitement of terror (which, dreadful as the idea is, I am obliged to confess I had actually felt), the sudden influx of life and strength to my brain, had pushed away for the moment the recollection of what lay outside. When I thought of it again, the blood began once more to course in my veins. Lecamus went on by my side with his head down, the eyelids drooping over his eyes, not saying a word. He followed me when I called him: but cast a regretful look at the postern by which we had gone out, through which I had dragged him back in a panic (I confess it) unworthy of me. Only when we had left at some distance behind us that door into the unseen, did my senses come fully back to me, and I ventured to ask myself what it meant. 'Lecamus, ' I said—I could scarcely put my question into words—'what do you think? what is your idea? —how do you explain—' Even then I am glad to think I had sufficient power of control not to betray all that I felt.

'One does not try to explain, ' he said slowly; 'one longs to know—that is all. If M. le Maire had not been—in such haste—had he been willing to go farther—to investigate——'

'God forbid! ' I said; and the impulse to quicken my steps, to get home and put myself in safety, was almost more than I could restrain. But I forced myself to go quietly, to measure my steps by his, which were slow and reluctant, as if he dragged himself away with difficulty from that which was behind.

What was it? 'Do not ask, do not ask! ' Nature seemed to say in my heart. Thoughts came into my mind in such a dizzy crowd, that the multitude of them seemed to take away my senses. I put up my hands to my ears, in which they seemed to be buzzing and rustling like bees, to stop the sound. When I did so, Lecamus turned and looked at me—grave and wondering. This recalled me to a sense of my weakness. But how I got home I can scarcely say. My mother and wife met me with anxiety. They were greatly disturbed about the hospital of St. Jean, in respect to which it had been recently decided that certain changes should be made. The great ward of the hospital, which was the chief establishment for the patients—a thing which some had complained of as an annoyance disturbing their rest. So many, indeed, had been the complaints received, that we had come to the conclusion either that the opening should be built up, or the office suspended. Against this decision, it is needless to say, the Sisters of St. Jean were moving heaven and earth. Equally unnecessary for me to add, that having so decided in my public capacity, as at once the representative of popular opinion and its guide, the covert reproaches which were breathed in my presence, and even the personal appeals made to me, had failed of any result. I respect the Sisters of St. Jean. They are good women and excellent nurses, and the commune owes them much. Still, justice must be impartial; and so long as I retain my position at the head of the community, it is my duty to see that all have their due. My opinions as a private individual, were I allowed to return to that humble position, are entirely a different matter; but this is a thing which ladies, however excellent, are slow to allow or to understand.

I will not pretend that this was to me a night of rest. In the darkness, when all is still, any anxiety which may afflict the soul is apt to gain complete possession and mastery, as all who have had true experience of life will understand. The night was very dark and very still, the clocks striking out the hours which went so slowly, and not another sound audible. The streets of Semur are always quiet, but they were more still than usual that night. Now and then, in a pause of my thoughts, I could hear the soft breathing of my Agnès in the adjoining room, which gave me a little comfort. But this was only by intervals, when I was able to escape from the grasp of the recollections that held me fast. Again I seemed to see under my closed eyelids the faint line of the high road which led from the Porte St. Lambert, the broken ground with its ragged bushes on either side, and no one—no one there—not a soul, not a shadow: yet a multitude! When I allowed myself to think of this, my heart leaped into my throat again, my blood ran in my veins like a river in flood. I need not say that I resisted this transport of the nerves with all my might. As the night grew slowly into morning my power of resistance increased; I turned my back, so to speak, upon my recollections, and said to myself, with growing firmness, that all sensations of the body must have their origin in the body. Some derangement of the system easily explainable, no doubt, if one but held the clue—must have produced the impression which otherwise it would be impossible to explain. As I turned this over and over in my mind, carefully avoiding all temptations to excitement—which is the only wise course in the case of a strong impression on the nerves—I gradually became able to believe that this was the cause. It is one of the penalties, I said to myself, which one has to pay for an organisation more finely tempered than that of the crowd.

This long struggle with myself made the night less tedious, though, perhaps, more terrible; and when at length I was overpowered by sleep, the short interval of unconsciousness restored me like a cordial. I woke in the early morning, feeling almost able to smile at the terrors of the night. When one can assure oneself that the day has really begun, even while it is yet dark, there is a change of sensation, an increase of strength and courage. One by one the dark hours went on. I heard them pealing from the Cathedral clock—four, five, six, seven—all dark, dark. I had got up and dressed before the last, but found no one else awake when I went out—no one stirring in the house, —no one moving in the street. The Cathedral doors were shut fast, a thing I have never seen before since I remember. Get up early who will, Père Laserques the sacristan is always up still earlier. He is a good old man, and I have often heard him say God's house should be open first of all houses, in case there might be any miserable ones about who had found no shelter in the dwellings of men. But the darkness had cheated even Père Laserques. To see those great doors closed which stood always open gave me a shiver, I cannot well tell why. Had they been open, there was an inclination in my mind to have gone in, though I cannot tell why; for I am not in the habit of attending mass, save on Sunday to set an example. There were no shops open, not a sound about. I went out upon the ramparts to the Mont St. Lambert, where the band plays on Sundays. In all the trees there was not so much as the twitter of a bird. I could hear the river flowing swiftly below the wall, but I could not see it, except as something dark, a ravine of gloom below, and beyond the walls I did not venture to look. Why should I look? There was nothing, nothing, as I knew. But fancy is so uncontrollable, and one's nerves so little to be trusted, that it was a wise precaution to refrain. The gloom itself was oppressive enough; the air seemed to creep with apprehensions, and from time to time my heart fluttered with a sick movement, as if it would escape from my control. But everything was still, still as the dead who had been so often in recent days called out of their graves by one or another. 'Enough to bring the dead out of their graves. ' What strange words to make use of! It was rather now as if the world had become a grave in which we, though living, were held fast.

Soon after this the dark world began to lighten faintly, and with the rising of a little white mist, like a veil rolling upwards, I at last saw the river and the fields beyond. To see anything at all lightened my heart a little, and I turned homeward when this faint daylight appeared. When I got back into the street, I found that the people at last were stirring. They had all a look of half panic, half shame upon their faces. Many were yawning and stretching themselves. 'Good morning, M. le Maire, ' said one and another; 'you are early astir. ' 'Not so early either, ' I said; and then they added, almost every individual, with a look of shame, 'We were so late this morning; we overslept ourselves—like yesterday. The weather is extraordinary. ' This was repeated to me by all kinds of people. They were half frightened, and they were ashamed. Père Laserques was sitting moaning on the Cathedral steps. Such a thing had never happened before. He had not rung the bell for early mass; he had not opened the Cathedral; he had not called M. le Curé. 'I think I must be going out of my senses, ' he said; 'but then, M. le Maire, the weather! Did anyone ever see such weather? I think there must be some evil brewing. It is not for nothing that the seasons change—that winter comes in the midst of summer. '

After this I went home. My mother came running to one door when I entered, and my wife to another. '*O mon fils!* ' and '*O mon ami!* ' they said, rushing upon me. They wept, these dear women. I could not at first prevail upon them to tell me what was the matter. At last they confessed that they believed something to have happened to me, in punishment for the wrong done to the Sisters at the hospital. 'Make haste, my son, to amend this error, ' my mother cried, 'lest a worse thing befall us! ' And then I discovered that among the women, and among many of the poor people, it had come to be believed that the darkness was a curse upon us for what we had done in respect to the hospital. This roused me to indignation. 'If they think I am to be driven from my duty by their magic, ' I cried; 'it is no better than witchcraft! ' not that I believed for a moment that it was they who had done it. My wife wept, and my mother became angry with me;

but when a thing is duty, it is neither wife nor mother who will move me out of my way.

It was a miserable day. There was not light enough to see anything—scarcely to see each other's faces; and to add to our alarm, some travellers arriving by the diligence (we are still three leagues from a railway, while that miserable little place, La Rochette, being the *chef-lieu,* has a terminus) informed me that the darkness only existed in Semur and the neighbourhood, and that within a distance of three miles the sun was shining. The sun was shining! was it possible? it seemed so long since we had seen the sunshine; but this made our calamity more mysterious and more terrible. The people began to gather into little knots in the streets to talk of the strange thing that was happening In the course of the day M. Barbou came to ask whether I did not think it would be well to appease the popular feeling by conceding what they wished to the Sisters of the hospital. I would not hear of it. 'Shall we own that we are in the wrong? I do not think we are in the wrong, ' I said, and I would not yield. 'Do you think the good Sisters have it in their power to darken the sky with their incantations? ' M. l'Adjoint shook his head. He went away with a troubled countenance; but then he was not like myself, a man of natural firmness. All the efforts that were employed to influence him were also employed with me; but to yield to the women was not in my thoughts.

We are now approaching, however, the first important incident in this narrative. The darkness increased as the afternoon came on; and it became a kind of thick twilight, no lighter than many a night. It was between five and six o'clock, just the time when our streets are the most crowded, when, sitting at my window, from which I kept a watch upon the Grande Rue, not knowing what might happen—I saw that some fresh incident had taken place. Very dimly through the darkness I perceived a crowd, which increased every moment, in front of the Cathedral. After watching it for a few minutes, I got my hat and went out. The people whom I saw—so many that they covered the whole middle of the *Place,* reaching almost to the pavement on the other side—had their heads all turned towards the Cathedral. 'What are you gazing at, my friend? ' I said to one by whom I stood. He looked up at me with a face which looked ghastly in the gloom. 'Look, M. le Maire! ' he said; 'cannot you see it on the great door? '

'I see nothing, ' said I; but as I uttered these words I did indeed see something which was very startling. Looking towards the great door of the Cathedral, as they all were doing, it suddenly seemed to me that I saw an illuminated placard attached to it, headed with the word *'Sommation'* in gigantic letters. *'Tiens! '* I cried; but when I looked again there was nothing. 'What is this? it is some witchcraft! ' I said, in spite of myself. 'Do you see anything, Jean Pierre? '

'M. le Maire, ' he said, 'one moment one sees something—the next, one sees nothing. Look! it comes again. ' I have always considered myself a man of courage, but when I saw this extraordinary appearance the panic which had seized upon me the former night returned, though in another form. Fly I could not, but I will not deny that my knees smote together. I stood for some minutes without being able to articulate a word—which, indeed, seemed the case with most of those before me. Never have I seen a more quiet crowd. They were all gazing, as if it was life or death that was set before them—while I, too, gazed with a shiver going over me. It was as I have seen an illumination of lamps in a stormy night; one moment the whole seems black as the wind sweeps over it, the next it springs into life again; and thus you go on, by turns losing and discovering the device formed by the lights. Thus from moment to moment there appeared before us, in letters that seemed to blaze and flicker, something that looked like a great official placard. *'Sommation! '*—this was how it was headed. I read a few words at a time, as it came and went; and who can describe the chill that ran through my veins as I made it out? It was a summons to the people of Semur by name—myself at the head as Maire (and I heard afterwards that every man who saw it saw his own name, though the whole *façade* of the Cathedral would not have held a full list of all the people of Semur)—to yield their places, which they had not filled aright, to those who knew the meaning of life, being dead. NOUS AUTRES MORTS—these were the words which blazed out oftenest of all, so that every one saw them. And 'Go! ' this terrible placard said—'Go! leave this place to us who know the true signification of life. ' These words I remember, but not the rest; and even at this moment it struck me that there was no explanation, nothing but this *vraie signification de la vie.* I felt like one in a dream: the light coming and going before me; one word, then another, appearing—sometimes a phrase like that I have quoted, blazing out, then dropping into darkness. For the moment I was struck dumb; but then it came back to my mind that I had an example to give, and that for me, eminently a man of my century, to yield credence to a miracle was something not to be thought of. Also I knew the necessity of doing something to break the impression of awe and terror on the mind of the people. 'This is a trick, ' I cried loudly, that all might hear. 'Let some one go and fetch M. de Clairon from the Musée. He will tell us how it has been done. ' This, boldly uttered, broke the spell. A number of pale faces gathered round me. 'Here is M. le Maire—he will clear it up, ' they cried, making room for me that I might approach nearer. 'M. le Maire is a man of courage—he has judgment. Listen to M. le Maire. ' It was a relief to everybody that I had spoken. And soon I found myself by the side of M. le Curé, who was standing among the rest, saying nothing, and with the air of one as much bewildered as any of us. He gave me one quick look from under his eyebrows to see who it was that approached him, as was his way, and made room for me, but said nothing. I was in too much emotion myself to keep silence—indeed, I was in that condition of wonder, alarm, and nervous excitement, that I had to speak or die; and there seemed an escape from something too terrible for flesh and blood to contemplate in the idea that there was trickery here. 'M. le Curé, ' I said, 'this is a strange ornament that you have placed on the front of your church. You are standing here to enjoy the effect. Now that you have seen how successful it has been, will not you tell me in confidence how it is done? '

I am conscious that there was a sneer in my voice, but I was too much excited to think of politeness. He gave me another of his rapid, keen looks.

'M. le Maire, ' he said, 'you are injurious to a man who is as little fond of tricks as yourself. '

His tone, his glance, gave me a certain sense of shame, but I could not stop myself. 'One knows, ' I said, 'that there are many things which an ecclesiastic may do without harm, which are not permitted to an ordinary layman—one who is an honest man, and no more. '

M. le Curé made no reply. He gave me another of his quick glances, with an impatient turn of his head. Why should I have suspected him? for no harm was known of him. He was the Curé, that was all; and perhaps we men of the world have our prejudices too. Afterwards, however, as we waited for M. de Clairon—for the crisis was too exciting for personal resentment—M. le Curé himself let drop something which made it apparent that it was the ladies of the hospital upon whom his suspicions fell. 'It is never well to offend women, M. le Maire, ' he said. 'Women do not discriminate the lawful from the unlawful: so long as they produce an effect, it does not matter to them. ' This gave me a strange impression, for it seemed to me that M. le Curé was abandoning his own side. However, all other sentiments were, as may be imagined, but as shadows compared with the overwhelming power that held all our eyes and our thoughts to the wonder before us. Every moment seemed an hour till M. de Clairon appeared. He was pushed forward through the crowd as by magic, all making room for him; and many of us thought that when science thus came forward capable of finding out everything, the miracle would disappear. But instead of this it seemed to glow brighter than ever. That great word '*Sommation*' blazed out, so that we saw his figure waver against the light as if giving way before the flames that scorched him. He was so near that his outline was marked out dark against the glare they gave. It was as though his close approach rekindled every light. Then, with a flicker and trembling, word by word and letter by letter went slowly out before our eyes.

M. de Clairon came down very pale, but with a sort of smile on his face. 'No, M. le Maire, ' he said, 'I cannot see how it is done. It is clever. I will examine the door further, and try the panels. Yes, I have left some one to watch that nothing is touched in the meantime, with the permission of M. le Curé—'

'You have my full permission, ' M. le Curé said; and M. de Clairon laughed, though he was still very pale. 'You saw my name there, ' he said. 'I am amused—I who am not one of your worthy citizens, M. le Maire. What can Messieurs les Morts of Semur want with a poor man of science like me? But you shall have my report before the evening is out. '

With this I had to be content. The darkness which succeeded to that strange light seemed more terrible than ever. We all stumbled as we turned to go away, dazzled by it, and stricken dumb, though some kept saying that it was a trick, and some murmured exclamations with voices full of terror. The sound of the crowd breaking up was like a regiment marching—all the world had been there. I was thankful, however, that neither my mother nor my wife had seen anything; and though they were anxious to know why I was so serious, I succeeded fortunately in keeping the secret from them.

M. de Clairon did not appear till late, and then he confessed to me he could make nothing of it. 'If it is a trick (as of course it must be), it has been most cleverly done, ' he said; and admitted that he was baffled altogether. For my part, I was not surprised. Had it been the Sisters of the hospital, as M. le Curé thought, would they have let the opportunity pass of preaching a sermon to us, and recommending their doctrines? Not so; here there were no doctrines, nothing but that pregnant phrase, *la vraie signification de la vie*. This made a more deep impression upon me than anything else. The Holy Mother herself (whom I wish to speak of with profound respect), and the saints, and the forgiveness of sins, would have all been there had it been the Sisters, or even M. le Curé. This, though I had myself suggested an imposture, made it very unlikely to my quiet thoughts. But if not an imposture, what could it be supposed to be?

EXPULSION OF THE INHABITANTS.

I will not attempt to give any detailed account of the state of the town during this evening. For myself I was utterly worn out, and went to rest as soon as M. de Clairon left me, having satisfied, as well as I could, the questions of the women. Even in the intensest excitement weary nature will claim her dues. I slept. I can even remember the grateful sense of being able to put all anxieties and perplexities aside for the moment, as I went to sleep. I felt the drowsiness gain upon me, and I was glad. To forget was of itself a happiness. I woke up, however, intensely awake, and in perfect possession of all my faculties, while it was yet dark; and at once got up and began to dress. The moment of hesitation which generally follows waking—the little interval of thought in which one turns over perhaps that which is past, perhaps that which is to come—found no place within me. I got up without a moment's pause, like one who has been called to go on a journey; nor did it surprise me at all to see my wife moving about, taking a cloak from her wardrobe, and putting up linen in a bag. She was already fully dressed; but she asked no questions of me any more than I did of her. We were in haste, though we said nothing. When I had dressed, I looked round me to see if I had forgotten anything, as one does when one leaves a place. I saw my watch suspended to its usual hook, and my pocketbook, which I had taken from my pocket on the previous night. I took up also the light overcoat which I had worn when I made my rounds through the city on the first night of the darkness. 'Now, ' I said, 'Agnès, I am ready. ' I did not speak to her of where we were going, nor she to me. Little Jean and my mother met us at the door. Nor did *she* say anything, contrary to her custom; and the child was quite quiet. We went downstairs together without saying a word. The servants, who were all astir, followed us. I cannot give any description of the feelings that were in my mind. I had not any feelings. I was only hurried out, hastened by something which I could not define—a sense that I must go; and perhaps I was too much astonished to do anything but yield. It seemed, however, to be no force or fear that was moving me, but a desire of my own; though I could not tell how it was, or why I should be so anxious to get away. All the servants, trooping after me, had the same look in their faces; they were anxious to be gone—it seemed their business to go—there was no question, no consultation. And when we came out into the street, we encountered a stream of processions similar to our own. The children went quite steadily by the side of their parents.

Little Jean, for example, on an ordinary occasion would have broken away—would have run to his comrades of the Bois-Sombre family, and they to him. But no; the little ones, like ourselves, walked along quite gravely. They asked no questions, neither did we ask any questions of each other, as, 'Where are you going? ' or, 'What is the meaning of a so-early promenade? ' Nothing of the kind; my mother took my arm, and my wife, leading little Jean by the hand, came to the other side. The servants followed. The street was quite full of people; but there was no noise except the sound of their footsteps. All of us turned the same way—turned towards the gates—and though I was not conscious of any feeling except the wish to go on, there were one or two things which took a place in my memory. The first was, that my wife suddenly turned round as we were coming out of the *porte-cochère*, her face lighting up. I need not say to any one who knows Madame Dupin de la Clairière, that she is a beautiful woman. Without any partiality on my part, it would be impossible for me to ignore this fact: for it is perfectly well known and acknowledged by all. She was pale this morning—a little paler than usual; and her blue eyes enlarged, with a serious look, which they always retain more or less. But suddenly, as we went out of the door, her face lighted up, her eyes were suffused with tears—with light—how can I tell what it was? —they became like the eyes of angels. A little cry came from her parted lips—she lingered a moment, stooping down as if talking to some one less tall than herself, then came after us, with that light still in her face. At the moment I was too much occupied to enquire what it was; but I noted it, even in the gravity of the occasion. The next thing I observed was M. le Curé, who, as I have already indicated, is a man of great composure of manner and presence of mind, coming out of the door of the Presbytery. There was a strange look on his face of astonishment and reluctance. He walked very slowly, not as we did, but with a visible desire to turn back, folding his arms across his breast, and holding himself as if against the wind, resisting some gale which blew behind him, and forced him on. We felt no gale; but there seemed to be a strange wind blowing along the side of the street on which M. le Curé was. And there was an air of concealed surprise in his face—great astonishment, but a determination not to let any one see that he was astonished, or that the situation was strange to him. And I cannot tell how it was, but I, too, though pre-occupied, was surprised to perceive that M. le Cure was going with the rest of us, though I could not have told why.

Behind M. le Curé there was another whom I remarked. This was Jacques Richard, he of whom I have already spoken. He was like a figure I have seen somewhere in sculpture. No one was near him, nobody touching him, and yet it was only necessary to look at the man to perceive that he was being forced along against his will. Every limb was in resistance; his feet were planted widely yet firmly upon the pavement; one of his arms was stretched out as if to lay hold on anything that should come within reach. M. le Curé resisted passively; but Jacques resisted with passion, laying his back to the wind, and struggling not to be carried away. Notwithstanding his resistance, however, this rough figure was driven along slowly, struggling at every step. He did not make one movement that was not against his will, but still he was driven on. On our side of the street all went, like ourselves, calmly. My mother uttered now and then a low moan, but said nothing. She clung to my arm, and walked on, hurrying a little, sometimes going quicker than I intended to go. As for my wife, she accompanied us with her light step, which scarcely seemed to touch the ground, little Jean pattering by her side. Our neighbours were all round us. We streamed down, as in a long procession, to the Porte St. Lambert. It was only when we got there that the strange character of the step we were all taking suddenly occurred to me. It was still a kind of grey twilight, not yet day. The bells of the Cathedral had begun to toll, which was very startling—not ringing in their cheerful way, but tolling as if for a funeral; and no other sound was audible but the noise of footsteps, like an army making a silent march into an enemy's country. We had reached the gate when a sudden wondering came over me. Why were we all going out of our houses in the wintry dusk to which our July days had turned? I stopped, and turning round, was about to say something to the others, when I became suddenly aware that here I was not my own master. My tongue clave to the root of my mouth; I could not say a word. Then I myself was turned round, and softly, firmly, irresistibly pushed out of the gate. My mother, who clung to me, added a little, no doubt, to the force against me, whatever it was, for she was frightened, and opposed herself to any endeavour on my part to regain freedom of movement; but all that her feeble force could do against mine must have been little. Several other men around me seemed to be moved as I was. M. Barbou, for one, made a still more decided effort to turn back, for, being a bachelor, he had no one to restrain him. Him I saw turned round as you would turn a *roulette*. He was thrown against my wife in his tempestuous course, and but that she was so light and elastic in her tread, gliding out straight and softly like one of the saints, I think he must have thrown her down. And at that moment, silent as we all were, his '*Pardon, Madame, mille pardons, Madame,* ' and his tone of horror at his own indiscretion, seemed to come to me like a voice out of another life. Partially roused before by the sudden impulse of resistance I have described, I was yet more roused now. I turned round, disengaging myself from my mother. 'Where are we going? why are we thus cast forth? My friends, help! ' I cried. I looked round upon the others, who, as I have said, had also awakened to a possibility of resistance. M. de Bois-Sombre, without a word, came and placed himself by my side; others started from the crowd. We turned to resist this mysterious impulse which had sent us forth. The crowd surged round us in the uncertain light.

Just then there was a dull soft sound, once, twice, thrice repeated. We rushed forward, but too late. The gates were closed upon us. The two folds of the great Porte St. Lambert, and the little postern for foot-passengers, all at once, not hurriedly, as from any fear of us, but slowly, softly, rolled on their hinges and shut—in our faces. I rushed forward with all my force and flung myself upon the gate. To what use? it was so closed as no mortal could open it. They told me after, for I was not aware at the moment, that I burst forth with cries and exclamations, bidding them 'Open, open in the name of God! ' I was not aware of what I said, but it seemed to me that I heard a voice of which nobody said anything to me, so that it would seem to have been unheard by the others, saying with a faint sound as of a trumpet, 'Closed—in the name of God. ' It might be only an echo, faintly brought back to me, of the words I had myself said.

There was another change, however, of which no one could have any doubt. When I turned round from these closed doors, though the moment before the darkness was such that we could not see the gates closing, I found the sun shining gloriously round us, and all my fellow-citizens turning with one impulse, with a sudden cry of joy, to hail the full day.

Le grand jour! Never in my life did I feel the full happiness of it, the full sense of the words before. The sun burst out into shining, the birds into singing. The sky stretched over us—deep and unfathomable and blue, —the grass grew under our feet, a soft air of morning blew upon us; waving the curls of the children, the veils of the women, whose faces were lit up by the beautiful day. After three days of darkness what a resurrection! It seemed to make up to us for the misery of being thus expelled from our homes. It was early, and all the freshness of the morning was upon the road and the fields, where the sun had just dried the dew. The river ran softly, reflecting the blue sky. How black it had been, deep and dark as a stream of ink, when I had looked down upon it from the Mont St. Lambert! and now it ran as clear and free as the voice of a little child. We all shared this moment of joy—for to us of the South the sunshine is as the breath of life, and to be deprived of it had been terrible. But when that first pleasure was over, the evidence of our strange position forced itself upon us with overpowering reality and force, made stronger by the very light. In the dimness it had not seemed so certain; now, gazing at each other in the clear light of the natural morning, we saw what had happened to us. No more delusion was possible. We could not flatter ourselves now that it was a trick or a deception. M. le Clairon stood there like the rest of us, staring at the closed gates which science could not open. And there stood M. le Curé, which was more remarkable still. The Church herself had not been able to do anything. We stood, a crowd of houseless exiles, looking at each other, our children clinging to us, our hearts failing us, expelled from our homes. As we looked in each other's faces we saw our own trouble. Many of the women sat down and wept; some upon the stones in the road, some on the grass. The children took fright from them, and began to cry too. What was to become of us? I looked round upon this crowd with despair in my heart. It was I to whom every one would look—for lodging, for direction—everything that human creatures want. It was my business to forget myself, though I also had been driven from my home and my city. Happily there was one thing I had left. In the pocket of my overcoat was my scarf of office. I stepped aside behind a tree, and took it out, and tied it upon me. That was something. There was thus a representative of order and law in the midst of the exiles, whatever might happen. This action, which a great number of the crowd saw, restored confidence. Many of the poor people gathered round me, and placed themselves near me, especially those women who had no natural support. When M. le Curé saw this, it seemed to make a great impression upon him. He changed colour, he who was usually so calm. Hitherto he had appeared bewildered, amazed to find himself as others. This, I must add, though you may perhaps think it superstitious, surprised me very much too. But now he regained his self-possession. He stepped upon a piece of wood that lay in front of the gate. 'My children'—he said. But just then the Cathedral bells, which had gone on tolling, suddenly burst into a wild peal. I do not know what it sounded like. It was a clamour of notes all run together, tone upon tone, without time or measure, as though a multitude had seized upon the bells and pulled all the ropes at once. If it was joy, what strange and terrible joy! It froze the very blood in our veins. M. le Curé became quite pale. He stepped down hurriedly from the piece of wood. We all made a hurried movement farther off from the gate.

It was now that I perceived the necessity of doing something, of getting this crowd disposed of, especially the women and the children. I am not ashamed to own that I trembled like the others; and nothing less than the consciousness that all eyes were upon me, and that my scarf of office marked me out among all who stood around, could have kept me from moving with precipitation as they did. I was enabled, however, to retire at a deliberate pace, and being thus slightly detached from the crowd, I took advantage of the opportunity to address them. Above all things, it was my duty to prevent a tumult in these unprecedented circumstances. 'My friends, ' I said, 'the event which has occurred is beyond explanation for the moment. The very nature of it is mysterious; the circumstances are such as require the closest investigation. But take courage. I pledge myself not to leave this place till the gates are open, and you can return to your homes; in the meantime, however, the women and the children cannot remain here. Let those who have friends in the villages near, go and ask for shelter; and let all who will, go to my house of La Clairière. My mother, my wife! recall to yourselves the position you occupy, and show an example. Lead our neighbours, I entreat you, to La Clairière. '

My mother is advanced in years and no longer strong, but she has a great heart. 'I will go, ' she said. 'God bless thee, my son! There will no harm happen; for if this be true which we are told, thy father is in Semur. '

There then occurred one of those incidents for which calculation never will prepare us. My mother's words seemed, as it were to open the flood-gates; my wife came up to me with the light in her face which I had seen when we left our own door. 'It was our little Marie—our angel, ' she said. And then there arose a great cry and clamour of others, both men and women pressing round. 'I saw my mother, ' said one, 'who is dead twenty years come the St. Jean. ' 'And I my little René, ' said another. 'And I my Camille, who was killed in Africa. ' And lo, what did they do, but rush towards the gate in a crowd—that gate from which they had but this moment fled in terror—beating upon it, and crying out, 'Open to us, open to us, our most dear! Do you think we have forgotten you? We have never forgotten you! ' What could we do with them, weeping thus, smiling, holding out their arms to—we knew not what? Even my Agnès was beyond my reach. Marie was our little girl who was dead. Those who were thus transported by a knowledge beyond ours were the weakest among us; most of them were women, the men old or feeble, and some children. I can recollect that I looked for Paul Lecamus among them, with wonder not to see him there. But though they were weak, they were beyond our strength to guide. What could we do with them? How could we force them away while they held to the fancy that those they loved were there? As it happens in times of emotion, it was those who were most impassioned who took the first place. We were at our wits' end.

But while we stood waiting, not knowing what to do, another sound suddenly came from the walls, which made them all silent in a moment. The most of us ran to this point and that (some taking flight altogether; but with the greater part anxious curiosity and anxiety had for the moment extinguished fear), in a wild eagerness to see who or what it was. But there was nothing to be seen, though the sound came from the wall close to the Mont St. Lambert, which I have already described. It was to me like the sound of a trumpet, and so I heard others say; and along with the trumpet were sounds as of words, though I could not make them out. But those others seemed to understand—they grew calmer—they ceased to weep. They raised their faces, all with that light upon them—that light I had seen in my Agnès. Some of them fell upon their knees. Imagine to yourself what a sight it was, all of us standing round, pale, stupefied, without a word to say! Then the women suddenly burst forth into replies—*'Oui, ma chérie! Oui, mon ange*! ' they cried. And while we looked they rose up; they came back, calling the children around them. My Agnès took that place which I had bidden her take. She had not hearkened to me, to leave me—but she hearkened now; and though I had bidden her to do this, yet to see her do it bewildered me, made my heart stand still. *'Mon ami,* ' she said, 'I must leave thee; it is commanded: they will not have the children suffer. ' What could we do? We stood pale and looked on, while all the little ones, all the feeble, were gathered in a little army. My mother stood like me—to her nothing had been revealed. She was very pale, and there was a quiver of pain in her lips. She was the one who had been ready to do my bidding: but there was a rebellion in her heart now. When the procession was formed (for it was my care to see that everything was done in order), she followed, but among the last. Thus they went away, many of them weeping, looking back, waving their hands to us. My Agnès covered her face, she could not look at me; but she obeyed. They went some to this side, some to that, leaving us gazing. For a long time we did nothing but watch them, going along the roads. What had their angels said to them? Nay, but God knows. I heard the sound; it was like the sound of the silver trumpets that travellers talk of; it was like music from heaven. I turned to M. le Curé, who was standing by. 'What is it? ' I cried, 'you are their director—you are an ecclesiastic—you know what belongs to the unseen. What is this that has been said to them? ' I have always thought well of M. le Curé. There were tears running down his cheeks.

'I know not, ' he said. 'I am a miserable like the rest. What they know is between God and them. Me! I have been of the world, like the rest.'

This is how we were left alone—the men of the city—to take what means were best to get back to our homes. There were several left among us who had shared the enlightenment of the women, but these were not persons of importance who could put themselves at the head of affairs. And there were women who remained with us, but these not of the best. To see our wives go was very strange to us; it was the thing we wished most to see, the women and children in safety; yet it was a strange sensation to see them go. For me, who had the charge of all on my hands, the relief was beyond description—yet was it strange; I cannot describe it. Then I called upon M. Barbou, who was trembling like a leaf, and gathered the chief of the citizens about me, including M. le Curé, that we should consult together what we should do.

I know no words that can describe our state in the strange circumstances we were now placed in. The women and the children were safe: that was much. But we—we were like an army suddenly formed, but without arms, without any knowledge of how to fight, without being able to see our enemy. We Frenchmen have not been without knowledge of such perils. We have seen the invader enter our doors; we have been obliged to spread our table for him, and give him of our best. But to be put forth by forces no man could resist—to be left outside, with the doors of our own houses closed upon us—to be confronted by nothing—by a mist, a silence, a darkness, —this was enough to paralyse the heart of any man. And it did so, more or less, according to the nature of those who were exposed to the trial. Some altogether failed us, and fled, carrying the news into the country, where most people laughed at there, as we understood afterwards. Some could do nothing but sit and gaze, huddled together in crowds, at the cloud over Semur, from which they expected to see fire burst and consume the city altogether. And a few, I grieve to say, took possession of the little *cabaret,* which stands at about half a kilometre from the St. Lambert gate, and established themselves there, in hideous riot, which was the worst thing of all for serious men to behold. Those upon whom I could rely I formed into patrols to go round the city, that no opening of a gate, or movement of those who were within, should take place without our knowledge. Such an emergency shows what men are. M. Barbou, though in ordinary times he discharges his duties as *adjoint* satisfactorily enough (though, it need not be added, a good Maire who is acquainted with his duties, makes the office of *adjoint* of but little importance), was now found entirely useless. He could not forget how he had been spun round and tossed forth from the city gates. When I proposed to put him at the head of a patrol, he had an attack of the nerves. Before nightfall he deserted me altogether, going off to his country-house, and taking a number of his neighbours with him. 'How can we tell when we may be permitted to return to the town? ' he said, with his teeth chattering. 'M. le Maire, I adjure you to put yourself in a place of safety. '

'Sir, ' I said to him, sternly, 'for one who deserts his post there is no place of safety. '

But I do not think he was capable of understanding me. Fortunately, I found in M. le Curé a much more trustworthy coadjutor. He was indefatigable; he had the habit of sitting up to all hours, of being called at all hours, in which our *bourgeoisie,* I cannot but acknowledge, is wanting. The expression I have before described of astonishment—but of astonishment which he wished to conceal—never left his face. He did not understand how such a thing could have been permitted to happen while he had no share in it; and, indeed, I will not deny that this was a matter of great wonder to myself too.

The arrangements I have described gave us occupation; and this had a happy effect upon us in distracting our minds from what had happened; for I think that if we had sat still and gazed at the dark city we should soon have gone mad, as some did. In our ceaseless patrols and attempts to find a way of entrance, we distracted ourselves from the enquiry, Who would dare to go in if the entrance were found? In the meantime not a gate was opened, not a figure was visible. We saw nothing, no more than if Semur had been a picture painted upon a canvas. Strange sights indeed met our eyes—sights which made even the bravest quail. The strangest of them was the boats that would go down and up the river, shooting forth from under the fortified bridge, which is one of the chief features of our town, sometimes with sails perfectly well managed, sometimes impelled by oars, but with no one visible in them—no one conducting them. To see one of these boats impelled up the stream, with no rower visible, was a wonderful sight. M. de Clairon, who was by my side, murmured something about a magnetic current; but when I asked him sternly by what set in motion, his voice died away in his moustache. M. le Curé said very little: one saw his lips move as he watched with us the passage of those boats. He smiled when it was proposed by some one to fire upon them. He read his Hours as he went round at the head of his patrol. My fellow townsmen and I conceived a great respect for him; and he inspired pity in me also. He had been the teacher of the Unseen among us, till the moment when the Unseen was thus, as it were, brought within our reach; but with the revelation he had nothing to do; and it filled him with pain and wonder. It made him silent; he said little about his religion, but signed himself, and his lips moved. He thought (I imagine) that he had displeased Those who are over all.

When night came the bravest of us were afraid. I speak for myself. It was bright moonlight where we were, and Semur lay like a blot between the earth and the sky, all dark: even the Cathedral towers were lost in it; nothing visible but the line of the ramparts, whitened outside by the moon. One knows what black and strange shadows are cast by the moonlight; and it seemed to all of us that we did not know what might be lurking behind every tree. The shadows of the branches looked like terrible faces. I sent all my people out on the patrols, though they were dropping with fatigue. Rather that than to be mad with terror. For myself, I took up my post as near the bank of the river as we could approach; for there was a limit beyond which we might not pass. I made the experiment often; and it seemed to me, and to all that attempted it, that we did reach the very edge of the stream; but the next moment perceived that we were at a certain distance, say twenty metres or thereabout. I placed myself there very often, wrapping a cloak about me to preserve me from the dew. (I may say that food had been sent us, and wine from La Clairière and many other houses in the neighbourhood, where the women had gone for this among other reasons, that we might be nourished by them.) And I must here relate a personal incident, though I have endeavoured not to be egotistical. While I sat watching, I distinctly saw a boat, a boat which belonged to myself, lying on the very edge of the shadow. The prow, indeed, touched the moonlight where it was cut clean across by the darkness; and this was how I discovered that it was the Marie, a pretty pleasure-boat which had been made for my wife. The sight of it made my heart beat; for what could it mean but that some one who was dear to me, some one in whom I took an interest, was there? I sprang up from where I sat to make another effort to get nearer; but my feet were as lead, and would not move; and there came a singing in my ears, and my blood coursed through my veins as in a fever. Ah! was it possible? I, who am a man, who have resolution, who have courage, who can lead the people, *I was afraid!* I sat down again and wept like a child. Perhaps it was my little Marie that was in the boat. God, He knows if I loved thee, my little angel! but I was afraid. O how mean is man! though we are so proud. They came near to me who were my own, and it was borne in upon my spirit that my good father was with the child; but because they had died I was afraid. I covered my face with my hands. Then it seemed to me that I heard a long quiver of a sigh; a long, long breath, such as sometimes relieves a sorrow that is beyond words. Trembling, I uncovered my eyes. There was nothing on the edge of the moonlight; all was dark, and all was still, the white radiance making a clear line across the river, but nothing more.

If my Agnès had been with me she would have seen our child, she would have heard that voice! The great cold drops of moisture were on my forehead. My limbs trembled, my heart fluttered in my bosom. I could neither listen nor yet speak. And those who would have spoken to me, those who loved me, sighing, went away. It is not possible that such wretchedness should be credible to noble minds; and if it had not been for pride and for shame, I should have fled away straight to La Clairière, to Put myself under shelter, to have some one near me who was less a coward than I. I, upon whom all the others relied, the Maire of the Commune! I make my confession. I was of no more force than this.

A voice behind me made me spring to my feet—the leap of a mouse would have driven me wild. I was altogether demoralised. 'Monsieur le Maire, it is but I, ' said some one quite humble and frightened.

'*Tiens!* —it is thou, Jacques! ' I said. I could have embraced him, though it is well known how little I approve of him. But he was living, he was a man like myself. I put out my hand, and felt him warm and breathing, and I shall never forget the ease that came to my heart. Its beating calmed. I was restored to myself.

'M. le Maire, ' he said, 'I wish to ask you something. Is it true all that is said about these people, I would say, these Messieurs? I do not wish to speak with disrespect, M. le Maire. '

'What is it, Jacques, that is said? ' I had called him 'thou' not out of contempt, but because, for the moment, he seemed to me as a brother, as one of my friends.

'M. le Maire, is it indeed *les morts* that are in Semur? '

He trembled, and so did I. 'Jacques, ' I said, 'you know all that I know. '

'Yes, M. le Maire, it is so, sure enough. I do not doubt it. If it were the Prussians, a man could fight. But *ces Messieurs l!* What I want to know is: is it because of what you did to those little Sisters, those good little ladies of St. Jean? '

'What I did? You were yourself one of the complainants. You were of those who said, when a man is ill, when he is suffering, they torment him with their mass; it is quiet he wants, not their mass. These were thy words, *vaurien*. And now you say it was I! '

'True, M. le Maire, ' said Jacques; 'but look you, when a man is better, when he has just got well, when he feels he is safe, then you should not take what he says for gospel. It would be strange if one had a new illness just when one is getting well of the old; and one feels now is the time to enjoy one's self, to kick up one's heels a little, while at least there is not likely to be much of a watch kept *up there*— the saints forgive me, ' cried Jacques, trembling and crossing himself, 'if I speak with levity at such a moment! And the little ladies were very kind. It was wrong to close their chapel, M. le Maire. From that comes all our trouble. '

'You good-for-nothing! ' I cried, 'it is you and such as you that are the beginning of our trouble. You thought there was no watch kept *up there*; you thought God would not take the trouble to punish you;

you went about the streets of Semur tossing a *grosse pièce* of a hundred sous, and calling out, "There is no God—this is my god; *l'argent, c'est le bon Dieu.*"'

'M. le Maire, M. le Maire, be silent, I implore you! It is enough to bring down a judgment upon us.'

'It has brought down a judgment upon us. Go thou and try what thy *grosse pièce* will do for thee now—worship thy god. Go, I tell you, and get help from your money.'

'I have no money, M. le Maire, and what could money do here? We would do much better to promise a large candle for the next festival, and that the ladies of St. Jean—'

'Get away with thee to the end of the world, thou and thy ladies of St. Jean!' I cried; which was wrong, I do not deny it, for they are good women, not like this good-for-nothing fellow. And to think that this man, whom I despise, was more pleasant to me than the dear souls who loved me! Shame came upon me at the thought. I too, then, was like the others, fearing the Unseen—capable of understanding only that which was palpable. When Jacques slunk away, which he did for a few steps, not losing sight of me, I turned my face towards the river and the town. The moonlight fell upon the water, white as silver where that line of darkness lay, shining, as if it tried, and tried in vain, to penetrate Semur; and between that and the blue sky overhead lay the city out of which we had been driven forth—the city of the dead. 'O God,' I cried, 'whom I know not, am not I to Thee as my little Jean is to me, a child and less than a child? Do not abandon me in this darkness. Would I abandon him were he ever so disobedient? And God, if thou art God, Thou art a better father than I.' When I had said this, my heart was a little relieved. It seemed to me that I had spoken to some one who knew all of us, whether we were dead or whether we were living. That is a wonderful thing to think of, when it appears to one not as a thing to believe, but as something that is real. It gave me courage. I got up and went to meet the patrol which was coming in, and found that great good-for-nothing Jacques running close after me, holding my cloak. 'Do not send me away, M. le Maire,' he said, 'I dare not stay by myself with *them* so near.' Instead of his money, in which he had trusted, it was I who had become his god now.

OUTSIDE THE WALLS.

There are few who have not heard something of the sufferings of a siege. Whether within or without, it is the most terrible of all the experiences of war. I am old enough to recollect the trenches before Sebastopol, and all that my countrymen and the English endured there. Sometimes I endeavoured to think of this to distract me from what we ourselves endured. But how different was it! We had neither shelter nor support. We had no weapons, nor any against whom to wield them. We were cast out of our homes in the midst of our lives, in the midst of our occupations, and left there helpless, to gaze at each other, to blind our eyes trying to penetrate the darkness before us. Could we have done anything, the oppression might have been less terrible—but what was there that we could do? Fortunately (though I do not deny that I felt each desertion) our band grew less and less every day. Hour by hour some one stole away—first one, then another, dispersing themselves among the villages near, in which many had friends. The accounts which these men gave were, I afterwards learnt, of the most vague description. Some talked of wonders they had seen, and were laughed at—and some spread reports of internal division among us. Not till long after did I know all the reports that went abroad. It was said that there had been fighting in Semur, and that we were divided into two factions, one of which had gained the mastery, and driven the other out. This was the story current in La Rochette, where they are always glad to hear anything to the discredit of the people of Semur; but no credence could have been given to it by those in authority, otherwise M. le Préfet, however indifferent to our interests, must necessarily have taken some steps for our relief. Our entire separation from the world was indeed one of the strangest details of this terrible period. Generally the diligence, though conveying on the whole few passengers, returned with two or three, at least, visitors or commercial persons, daily-and the latter class frequently arrived in carriages of their own; but during this period no stranger came to see our miserable plight. We made shelter for ourselves under the branches of the few trees that grew in the uncultivated ground on either side of the road—and a hasty erection, half tent half shed, was put up for a place to assemble in, or for those who were unable to bear the heat of the day or the occasional chills of the night. But the most of us were too restless to seek repose, and could not bear to be out of sight of the city. At any moment it seemed to us the gates might open, or some loophole be visible by which we might throw ourselves upon the darkness and vanquish it. This was what we said to ourselves, forgetting how we shook and trembled whenever any contact had been possible with those who were within. But one thing was certain, that though we feared, we could not turn our eyes from the place. We slept leaning against a tree, or with our heads on our hands, and our faces toward Semur. We took no count of day or night, but ate the morsel the women brought to us, and slept thus, not sleeping, when want or weariness overwhelmed us. There was scarcely an hour in the day that some of the women did not come to ask what news. They crept along the roads in twos and threes, and lingered for hours sitting by the way weeping, starting at every breath of wind.

Meanwhile all was not silent within Semur. The Cathedral bells rang often, at first filling us with hope, for how familiar was that sound! The first time, we all gathered together and listened, and many wept. It was as if we heard our mother's voice. M. de Bois-Sombre burst into tears. I have never seen him within the doors of the Cathedral since his marriage; but he burst into tears. '*Mon Dieu!* if I were but there! ' he said. We stood and listened, our hearts melting, some falling on their knees. M. le Curé stood up in the midst of us and began to intone the psalm: [He has a beautiful voice. It is sympathetic, it goes to the heart.] 'I was glad when they said to me, Let us go up—' And though there were few of us who could have supposed themselves capable of listening to that sentiment a little while before with any sympathy, yet a vague hope rose up within us while we heard him, while we listened to the bells. What man is there to whom the bells of his village, the *carillon* of his city, is not most dear? It rings for him through all his life; it is the first sound of home in the distance when he comes back—the last that follows him like a long farewell when he goes away. While we listened, we forgot our fears. They were as we were, they were also our brethren, who rang those bells. We seemed to see them trooping into our beautiful Cathedral. All! only to see it again, to be within its shelter, cool and calm as in our mother's arms! It seemed to us that we should wish for nothing more.

When the sound ceased we looked into each other's faces, and each man saw that his neighbour was pale. Hope died in us when the sound died away, vibrating sadly through the air. Some men threw themselves on the ground in their despair.

And from this time forward many voices were heard, calls and shouts within the walls, and sometimes a sound like a trumpet, and other instruments of music. We thought, indeed, that noises as of bands patrolling along the ramparts were audible as our patrols worked their way round and round. This was a duty which I never allowed to be neglected, not because I put very much faith in it, but because it gave us a sort of employment. There is a story somewhere which I recollect dimly of an ancient city which its assailants did not touch, but only marched round and round till the walls fell, and they could enter. Whether this was a story of classic times or out of our own remote history, I could not recollect. But I thought of it many times while we made our way like a procession of ghosts, round and round, straining our ears to hear what those voices were which sounded above us, in tones that were familiar, yet so strange. This story got so much into my head (and after a time all our heads seemed to get confused and full of wild and bewildering expedients) that I found myself suggesting—I, a man known for sense and reason—that we should blow trumpets at some time to be fixed, which was a thing the ancients had done in the strange tale which had taken possession of me. M. le Curé looked at me with disapproval. He said, 'I did not expect from M. le Maire anything that was disrespectful to religion. ' Heaven forbid that I should be disrespectful to religion at any time of life, but then it was impossible to me. I remembered after that the tale of which I speak, which had so seized upon me, was in the sacred writings; but those who know me will understand that no sneer at these writings or intention of wounding the feelings of M. le Curé was in my mind.

I was seated one day upon a little inequality of the ground, leaning my back against a half-withered hawthorn, and dozing with my head in my hands, when a soothing, which always diffuses itself from her presence, shed itself over me, and opening my eyes, I saw my Agnès sitting by me. She had come with some food and a little linen, fresh and soft like her own touch. My wife was not gaunt and worn like me, but she was pale and as thin as a shadow. I woke with a start, and seeing her there, there suddenly came a dread over me that she would pass away before my eyes, and go over to Those who were within Semur. I cried '*Non, mon Agnès; non, mon Agnès:* before you ask, No! ' seizing her and holding her fast in this dream, which was not altogether a dream. She looked at me with a smile, that smile that has always been to me as the rising of the sun over the earth.

'*Mon ami,* ' she said surprised, 'I ask nothing, except that you should take a little rest and spare thyself. ' Then she added, with haste, what I knew she would say, 'Unless it were this, *mon ami*. If I were permitted, I would go into the city—I would ask those who are there what is their meaning: and if no way can be found—no act of penitence. —Oh! do not answer in haste! I have no fear; and it would be to save thee. '

A strong throb of anger came into my throat. Figure to yourself that I looked at my wife with anger, with the same feeling which had moved me when the deserters left us; but far more hot and sharp. I seized her soft hands and crushed them in mine. 'You would leave me! ' I said. 'You would desert your husband. You would go over to our enemies! '

'O Martin, say not so, ' she cried, with tears. 'Not enemies. There is our little Marie, and my mother, who died when I was born. '

'You love these dead tyrants. Yes, ' I said, 'you love them best. You will go to—the majority, to the strongest. Do not speak to me! Because your God is on their side, you will forsake us too. '

Then she threw herself upon me and encircled me with her arms. The touch of them stilled my passion; but yet I held her, clutching her gown, so terrible a fear came over me that she would go and come back no more.

'Forsake thee! ' she breathed out over me with a moan. Then, putting her cool cheek to mine, which burned, 'But I would die for thee, Martin. '

'Silence, my wife: that is what you shall not do, ' I cried, beside myself. I rose up; I put her away from me. That is, I know it, what has been done. Their God does this, they do not hesitate to say—takes from you what you love best, to make you better—*you!* and they ask you to love Him when He has thus despoiled you! 'Go home, Agnès, ' I said, hoarse with terror. 'Let us face them as we may; you shall not go among them, or put thyself in peril. Die for me! *Mon Dieu!* and what then, what should I do then? Turn your face from them; turn from them; go! go! and let me not see thee here again. '

My wife did not understand the terror that seized me. She obeyed me, as she always does, but, with the tears falling from her white cheeks, fixed upon me the most piteous look. '*Mon ami,* ' she said, 'you are disturbed, you are not in possession of yourself; this cannot be what you mean. '

'Let me not see thee here again! ' I cried. 'Would you make me mad in the midst of my trouble? No! I will not have you look that way. Go home! go home! ' Then I took her into my arms and wept, though I am not a man given to tears. 'Oh! my Agnès, ' I said, 'give me thy counsel. What you tell me I will do; but rather than risk thee, I would live thus for ever, and defy them. '

She put her hand upon my lips. 'I will not ask this again, ' she said, bowing her head; 'but defy them—why should you defy them? Have they come for nothing? Was Semur a city of the saints? They have come to convert our people, Martin—thee too, and the rest. If you will submit your hearts, they will open the gates, they will go back to their sacred homes and we to ours. This has been borne in upon me sleeping and waking; and it seemed to me that if I could but go, and say, "Oh! my fathers, oh! my brothers, they submit, " all would be well. For I do not fear them, Martin. Would they harm me that love us? I would but give our Marie one kiss— —'

'You are a traitor! ' I said. 'You would steal yourself from me, and do me the worst wrong of all— —'

But I recovered my calm. What she said reached my understanding at last. 'Submit! ' I said, 'but to what? To come and turn us from our homes, to wrap our town in darkness, to banish our wives and our children, to leave us here to be scorched by the sun and drenched by the rain, —this is not to convince us, my Agnès. And to what then do you bid us submit— —? '

'It is to convince you, *mon ami,* of the love of God, who has permitted this great tribulation to be, that we might be saved, ' said Agnès. Her face was sublime with faith. It is possible to these dear women; but for me the words she spoke were but words without meaning. I shook my head. Now that my horror and alarm were passed, I could well remember often to have heard words like these before.

'My angel! ' I said, 'all this I admire, I adore in thee; but how is it the love of God? —and how shall we be saved by it? Submit! I will do anything that is reasonable; but of what truth have we here the proof——? '

Some one had come up behind as we were talking. When I heard his voice I smiled, notwithstanding my despair. It was natural that the Church should come to the woman's aid. But I would not refuse to give ear to M. le Curé, who had proved himself a man, had he been ten times a priest.

'I have not heard what Madame has been saying, M. le Maire, neither would I interpose but for your question. You ask of what truth have we the proof here? It is the Unseen that has revealed itself. Do we see anything, you and I? Nothing, nothing, but a cloud. But that which we cannot see, that which we know not, that which we dread—look! it is there. '

I turned unconsciously as he pointed with his hand. Oh, heaven, what did I see! Above the cloud that wrapped Semur there was a separation, a rent in the darkness, and in mid heaven the Cathedral towers, pointing to the sky. I paid no more attention to M. le Curé. I sent forth a shout that roused all, even the weary line of the patrol that was marching slowly with bowed heads round the walls; and there went up such a cry of joy as shook the earth. 'The towers, the towers! ' I cried. These were the towers that could be seen leagues off, the first sign of Semur; our towers, which we had been born to love like our father's name. I have had joys in my life, deep and great. I have loved, I have won honours, I have conquered difficulty; but never had I felt as now. It was as if one had been born again.

When we had gazed upon them, blessing them and thanking God, I gave orders that all our company should be called to the tent, that we might consider whether any new step could now be taken: Agnès with the other women sitting apart on one side and waiting. I recognised even in the excitement of such a time that theirs was no easy part. To sit there silent, to wait till we had spoken, to be bound by what we decided, and to have no voice—yes, that was hard. They thought they knew better than we did: but they were silent, devouring us with their eager eyes. I love one woman more than all the world; I count her the best thing that God has made; yet would I not be as Agnès for all that life could give me. It was her part to be silent, and she was so, like the angel she is, while even Jacques Richard had the right to speak. *Mon Dieu!* but it is hard, I allow it; they have need to be angels. This thought passed through my mind even at the crisis which had now arrived. For at such moments one sees everything, one thinks of everything, though it is only after that one remembers what one has seen and thought. When my fellow-citizens gathered together (we were now less than a hundred in number, so many had gone from us), I took it upon myself to speak. We were a haggard, worn-eyed company, having had neither shelter nor sleep nor even food, save in hasty snatches. I stood at the door of the tent and they below, for the ground sloped a little. Beside me were M. le Curé, M. de Bois-Sombre, and one or two others of the chief citizens. 'My friends, ' I said, 'you have seen that a new circumstance has occurred. It is not within our power to tell what its meaning is, yet it must be a symptom of good. For my own part, to see these towers makes the air lighter. Let us think of the Church as we may, no one can deny that the towers of Semur are dear to our hearts. '

'M. le Maire, ' said M. de Bois-Sombre, interrupting, 'I speak I am sure the sentiments of my fellow-citizens when I say that there is no longer any question among us concerning the Church; it is an admirable institution, a universal advantage——'

'Yes, yes, ' said the crowd, 'yes, certainly! ' and some added, 'It is the only safeguard, it is our protection, ' and some signed themselves. In the crowd I saw Riou, who had done this at the *octroi*. But the sign did not surprise me now.

M. le Curé stood by my side, but he did not smile. His countenance was dark, almost angry. He stood quite silent, with his eyes on the ground. It gave him no pleasure, this profession of faith.

'It is well, my friends, ' said I, 'we are all in accord; and the good God has permitted us again to see these towers. I have called you together to collect your ideas. This change must have a meaning. It has been suggested to me that we might send an ambassador—a messenger, if that is possible, into the city—'

Here I stopped short; and a shiver ran through me—a shiver which went over the whole company. We were all pale as we looked in each other's faces; and for a moment no one ventured to speak. After this pause it was perhaps natural that he who first found his voice should be the last who had any right to give an opinion. Who should it be but Jacques Richard? 'M. le Maire, ' cried the fellow, 'speaks at his ease—but who will thus risk himself? ' Probably he did not mean that his grumbling should be heard, but in the silence every sound was audible; there was a gasp, a catching of the breath, and all turned their eyes again upon me. I did not pause to think what answer I should give. 'I! ' I cried. 'Here stands one who will risk himself, who will perish if need be—'

Something stirred behind me. It was Agnès who had risen to her feet, who stood with her lips parted and quivering, with her hands clasped, as if about to speak. But she did not speak. Well! she had proposed to do it. Then why not I?

'Let me make the observation, ' said another of our fellow-citizens, Bordereau the banker, 'that this would not be just. Without M. le Maire we should be a mob without a head. If a messenger is to be sent, let it be some one not so indispensable——'

'Why send a messenger? ' said another, Philip Leclerc. 'Do we know that these Messieurs will admit any one? and how can you speak, how can you parley with those—' and he too, was seized with a shiver—'whom you cannot see? '

Then there came another voice out of the crowd. It was one who would not show himself, who was conscious of the mockery in his tone. 'If there is any one sent, let it be M. le Curé, ' it said.

M. le Curé stepped forward. His pale countenance flushed red. 'Here am I, ' he said, 'I am ready; but he who spoke speaks to mock me. Is it befitting in this presence? '

There was a struggle among the men. Whoever it was who had spoken (I did not wish to know), I had no need to condemn the mocker; they themselves silenced him; then Jacques Richard (still less worthy of credit) cried out again with a voice that was husky. What are men made of? Notwithstanding everything, it was from the *cabaret*, from the wine-shop, that he had come. He said, 'Though M. le Maire will not take my opinion, yet it is this. Let them reopen the chapel in the hospital. The ladies of St. Jean—'

'Hold thy peace, ' I said, 'miserable! ' But a murmur rose. 'Though it is not his part to speak, I agree, ' said one. 'And I. ' 'And I. ' There was well-nigh a tumult of consent; and this made me angry. Words were on my lips which it might have been foolish to utter, when M. de Bois-Sombre, who is a man of judgment, interfered.

'M. le Maire,' he said, 'as there are none of us here who would show disrespect to the Church and holy things—that is understood—it is not necessary to enter into details. Every restriction that would wound the most susceptible is withdrawn; not one more than another, but all. We have been indifferent in the past, but for the future you will agree with me that everything shall be changed. The ambassador—whoever he may be—' he added with a catching of his breath, 'must be empowered to promise—everything—submission to all that may be required.'

Here the women could not restrain themselves; they all rose up with a cry, and many of them began to weep. 'Ah!' said one with a hysterical sound of laughter in her tears. '*Sainte Mère*! it will be heaven upon earth.'

M. le Curé said nothing; a keen glance of wonder, yet of subdued triumph, shot from under his eyelids. As for me, I wrung my hands: 'What you say will be superstition; it will be hypocrisy,' I cried.

But at that moment a further incident occurred. Suddenly, while we deliberated, a long loud peal of a trumpet sounded into the air. I have already said that many sounds had been heard before; but this was different; there was not one of us that did not feel that this was addressed to himself. The agitation was extreme; it was a summons, the beginning of some distinct communication. The crowd scattered; but for myself, after a momentary struggle, I went forward resolutely. I did not even look back at my wife. I was no longer Martin Dupin, but the Maire of Semur, the saviour of the community. Even Bois-Sombre quailed: but I felt that it was in me to hold head against death itself; and before I had gone two steps I felt rather than saw that M. le Curé had come to my side. We went on without a word; gradually the others collected behind us, following yet straggling here and there upon the inequalities of the ground.

Before us lay the cloud that was Semur, a darkness defined by the shining of the summer day around, the river escaping from that gloom as from a cavern, the towers piercing through, but the sunshine thrown back on every side from that darkness. I have spoken of the walls as if we saw them, but there were no walls visible, nor any gate, though we all turned like blind men to where the Porte St. Lambert was. There was the broad vacant road leading up to it, leading into the gloom. We stood there at a little distance. Whether it was human weakness or an invisible barrier, how can I tell? We stood thus immovable, with the trumpet pealing out over us, out of the cloud. It summoned every man as by his name. To me it was not wonderful that this impression should come, but afterwards it was elicited from all that this was the feeling of each. Though no words were said, it was as the calling of our names. We all waited in such a supreme agitation as I cannot describe for some communication that was to come.

When suddenly, in a moment, the trumpet ceased; there was an interval of dead and terrible silence; then, each with a leap of his heart as if it would burst from his bosom, we saw a single figure slowly detach itself out of the gloom. 'My God! ' I cried. My senses went from me; I felt my head go round like a straw tossed on the winds.

To know them so near, those mysterious visitors—to feel them, to hear them, was not that enough? But, to see! who could bear it? Our voices rang like broken chords, like a tearing and rending of sound. Some covered their faces with their hands; for our very eyes seemed to be drawn out of their sockets, fluttering like things with a separate life.

Then there fell upon us a strange and wonderful calm. The figure advanced slowly; there was weakness in it. The step, though solemn, was feeble; and if you can figure to yourself our consternation, the pause, the cry—our hearts dropping back as it might be into their places—the sudden stop of the wild panting in our breasts: when there became visible to us a human face well known, a man as we were. 'Lecamus! ' I cried; and all the men round took it up, crowding nearer, trembling yet delivered from their terror; some even laughed in the relief. There was but one who had an air of discontent, and that was M. le Curé. As he said 'Lecamus! ' like the rest, there was impatience, disappointment, anger in his tone.

And I, who had wondered where Lecamus had gone; thinking sometimes that he was one of the deserters who had left us! But when he came nearer his face was as the face of a dead man, and a cold chill came over us. His eyes, which were cast down, flickered under the thin eyelids in which all the veins were visible. His face was gray like that of the dying. 'Is he dead? ' I said. But, except M. le Curé, no one knew that I spoke.

'Not even so, ' said M. le Cure, with a mortification in his voice, which I have never forgotten. 'Not even so. That might be something. They teach us not by angels—by the fools and offscourings of the earth. '

And he would have turned away. It was a humiliation. Was not he the representative of the Unseen, the vice-gerent, with power over heaven and hell? but something was here more strong than he. He stood by my side in spite of himself to listen to the ambassador. I will not deny that such a choice was strange, strange beyond measure, to me also.

'Lecamus, ' I said, my voice trembling in my throat, 'have you been among the dead, and do you live? '

'I live, ' he said; then looked around with tears upon the crowd. 'Good neighbours, good friends, ' he said, and put out his hand and touched them; he was as much agitated as they.

'M. Lecamus, ' said I, 'we are here in very strange circumstances, as you know; do not trifle with us. If you have indeed been with those who have taken the control of our city, do not keep us in suspense. You will see by the emblems of my office that it is to me you must address yourself; if you have a mission, speak. '

'It is just, ' he said, 'it is just—but bear with me one moment. It is good to behold those who draw breath; if I have not loved you enough, my good neighbours, forgive me now! '

'Rouse yourself, Lecamus, ' said I with some anxiety. 'Three days we have been suffering here; we are distracted with the suspense. Tell us your message—if you have anything to tell. '

'Three days! ' he said, wondering; 'I should have said years. Time is long when there is neither night nor day. ' Then, uncovering himself, he turned towards the city. 'They who have sent me would have you know that they come, not in anger but in friendship: for the love they bear you, and because it has been permitted——'

As he spoke his feebleness disappeared. He held his head high; and we clustered closer and closer round him, not losing a half word, not a tone, not a breath.

'They are not the dead. They are the immortal. They are those who dwell—elsewhere. They have other work, which has been interrupted because of this trial. They ask, "Do you know now—do you know now? " this is what I am bidden to say. '

'What'—I said (I tried to say it, but my lips were dry), 'What would they have us to know? '

But a clamour interrupted me. 'Ah! yes, yes, yes! ' the people cried, men and women; some wept aloud, some signed themselves, some held up their hands to the skies. 'Nevermore will we deny religion, ' they cried, 'never more fail in our duties. They shall see how we will follow every office, how the churches shall be full, how we will observe the feasts and the days of the saints! M. Lecamus, ' cried two or three together; 'go, tell these Messieurs that we will have masses said for them, that we will obey in everything. We have seen what comes of it when a city is without piety. Never more will we neglect the holy functions; we will vow ourselves to the holy Mother and the saints—'

'And if those ladies wish it, ' cried Jacques Richard, 'there shall be as many masses as there are priests to say them in the Hospital of St. Jean. '

'Silence, fellow! ' I cried; 'is it for you to promise in the name of the Commune? ' I was almost beside myself. 'M. Lecamus. is it for this that they have come? '

His head had begun to droop again, and a dimness came over his face. 'Do I know? ' he said. 'It was them I longed for, not to know their errand; but I have not yet said all. You are to send two—two whom you esteem the highest—to speak with them face to face. '

Then at once there rose a tumult among the people—an eagerness which nothing could subdue. There was a cry that the ambassadors were already elected, and we were pushed forward, M. le Curé and myself, towards the gate. They would not hear us speak. 'We promise, ' they cried, 'we promise everything; let us but get back. ' Had it been to sacrifice us they would have done the same; they would have killed us in their passion, in order to return to their city—and afterwards mourned us and honoured us as martyrs. But for the moment they had neither ruth nor fear. Had it been they who were going to reason not with flesh and blood, it would have been different; but it was we, not they; and they hurried us on as not willing that a moment should be lost. I had to struggle, almost to fight, in order to provide them with a leader, which was indispensable, before I myself went away. For who could tell if we should ever come back? For a moment I hesitated, thinking that it might be well to invest M. de Bois-Sombre as my deputy with my scarf of office; but then I reflected that when a man goes to battle, when he goes to risk his life, perhaps to lose it, for his people, it is his right to bear those signs which distinguish him from common men, which show in what office, for what cause, he is ready to die.

Accordingly I paused, struggling against the pressure of the people, and said in a loud voice, 'In the absence of M. Barbou, who has forsaken us, I constitute the excellent M. Felix de Bois-Sombre my representative. In my absence my fellow-citizens will respect and obey him as myself. ' There was a cry of assent. They would have given their assent to anything that we might but go on. What was it to them? They took no thought of the heaving of my bosom, the beating of my heart. They left us on the edge of the darkness with our faces towards the gate. There we stood one breathless moment. Then the little postern slowly opened before us, and once more we stood within Semur.

THE NARRATIVE OF PAUL LECAMUS.

M. le Maire having requested me, on his entrance into Semur, to lose no time in drawing up an account of my residence in the town, to be placed with his own narrative, I have promised to do so to the best of my ability, feeling that my condition is a very precarious one, and my time for explanation may be short. Many things, needless to enumerate, press this upon my mind. It was a pleasure to me to see my neighbours when I first came out of the city; but their voices, their touch, their vehemence and eagerness wear me out. From my childhood up I have shrunk from close contact with my fellow-men. My mind has been busy with other thoughts; I have desired to investigate the mysterious and unseen. When I have walked abroad I have heard whispers in the air; I have felt the movement of wings, the gliding of unseen feet. To my comrades these have been a source of alarm and disquiet, but not to me; is not God in the unseen with all His angels? and not only so, but the best and wisest of men. There was a time indeed, when life acquired for me a charm. There was a smile which filled me with blessedness, and made the sunshine more sweet. But when she died my earthly joys died with her. Since then I have thought of little but the depths profound, into which she has disappeared like the rest.

I was in the garden of my house on that night when all the others left Semur. I was restless, my mind was disturbed. It seemed to me that I approached the crisis of my life. Since the time when I led M. le Maire beyond the walls, and we felt both of us the rush and pressure of that crowd, a feeling of expectation had been in my mind. I knew not what I looked for—but something I looked for that should change the world. The 'Sommation' on the Cathedral doors did not surprise me. Why should it be a matter of wonder that the dead should come back? the wonder is that they do not. Ah! that is the wonder. How one can go away who loves you, and never return, nor speak, nor send any message—that is the miracle: not that the heavens should bend down and the gates of Paradise roll back, and those who have left us return. All my life it has been a marvel to me how they could be kept away. I could not stay in-doors on this strange night. My mind was full of agitation. I came out into the garden though it was dark. I sat down upon the bench under the trellis—she loved it. Often had I spent half the night there thinking of her.

It was very dark that night: the sky all veiled, no light anywhere a night like November. One would have said there was snow in the air. I think I must have slept toward morning (I have observed throughout that the preliminaries of these occurrences have always been veiled in sleep), and when I woke suddenly it was to find myself, if I may so speak, the subject of a struggle. The struggle was within me, yet it was not I. In my mind there was a desire to rise from where I sat and go away, I could not tell where or why; but something in me said stay, and my limbs were as heavy as lead. I could not move; I sat still against my will; against one part of my will—but the other was obstinate and would not let me go. Thus a combat took place within me of which I knew not the meaning. While it went on I began to hear the sound of many feet, the opening of doors, the people pouring out into the streets. This gave me no surprise; it seemed to me that I understood why it was; only in my own case, I knew nothing. I listened to the steps pouring past, going on and on, faintly dying away in the distance, and there was a great stillness. I then became convinced, though I cannot tell how, that I was the only living man left in Semur; but neither did this trouble me. The struggle within me came to an end, and I experienced a great calm.

I cannot tell how long it was till I perceived a change in the air, in the darkness round me. It was like the movement of some one unseen. I have felt such a sensation in the night, when all was still, before now. I saw nothing. I heard nothing. Yet I was aware, I cannot tell how, that there was a great coming and going, and the sensation as of a multitude in the air. I then rose and went into my house, where Leocadie, my old housekeeper, had shut all the doors so carefully when she went to bed. They were now all open, even the door of my wife's room of which I kept always the key, and where no one entered but myself; the windows also were open. I looked out upon the Grande Rue, and all the other houses were like mine. Everything was open, doors and windows, and the streets were full. There was in them a flow and movement of the unseen, without a sound, sensible only to the soul. I cannot describe it, for I neither heard nor saw, but felt. I have often been in crowds; I have lived in Paris, and once passed into England, and walked about the London streets. But never, it seemed to me, never was I aware of so many, of so great a multitude. I stood at my open window, and watched as in a dream. M. le Maire is aware that his house is visible from mine. Towards that a stream seemed to be always going, and at the windows and in the doorways was a sensation of multitudes like that which I have already described. Gazing out thus upon the revolution which was happening before my eyes, I did not think of my own house or what was passing there, till suddenly, in a moment, I was aware that some one had come in to me. Not a crowd as elsewhere; one. My heart leaped up like a bird let loose; it grew faint within me with joy and fear. I was giddy so that I could not stand. I called out her name, but low, for I was too happy, I had no voice. Besides was it needed, when heart already spoke to heart?

I had no answer, but I needed none. I laid myself down on the floor where her feet would be. Her presence wrapped me round and round. It was beyond speech. Neither did I need to see her face, nor to touch her hand. She was more near to me, more near, than when I held her in my arms. How long it was so, I cannot tell; it was long as love, yet short as the drawing of a breath. I knew nothing, felt nothing but Her, alone; all my wonder and desire to know departed from me. We said to each other everything without words—heart overflowing into heart. It was beyond knowledge or speech.

But this is not of public signification that I should occupy with it the time of M. le Maire.

After a while my happiness came to an end. I can no more tell how, than I can tell how it came. One moment, I was warm in her presence; the next, I was alone. I rose up staggering with blindness and woe—could it be that already, already it was over? I went out blindly following after her. My God, I shall follow, I shall follow, till life is over. She loved me; but she was gone.

Thus, despair came to me at the very moment when the longing of my soul was satisfied and I found myself among the unseen; but I cared for knowledge no longer, I sought only her. I lost a portion of my time so. I regret to have to confess it to M. le Maire. Much that I might have learned will thus remain lost to my fellow-citizens and the world. We are made so. What we desire eludes us at the moment of grasping it—or those affections which are the foundation of our lives preoccupy us, and blind the soul. Instead of endeavouring to establish my faith and enlighten my judgment as to those mysteries which have been my life-long study, all higher purpose departed from me; and I did nothing but rush through the city, groping among those crowds, seeing nothing, thinking of nothing—save of One.

From this also I awakened as out of a dream. What roused me was the pealing of the Cathedral bells. I was made to pause and stand still, and return to myself. Then I perceived, but dimly, that the thing which had happened to me was that which I had desired all my life. I leave this explanation of my failure [Footnote: The reader will remember that the ringing of the Cathedral bells happened in fact very soon after the exodus of the citizens; so that the self-reproaches of M. Lecamus had less foundation than he thought.] in public duty to the charity of M. le Maire.

The bells of the Cathedral brought me back to myself—to that which we call reality in our language; but of all that was around me when I regained consciousness, it now appeared to me that I only was a dream. I was in the midst of a world where all was in movement. What the current was which flowed around me I know not; if it was thought which becomes sensible among spirits, if it was action, I cannot tell. But the energy, the force, the living that was in them, that could no one misunderstand. I stood in the streets, lagging and feeble, scarcely able to wish, much less to think. They pushed against me, put me aside, took no note of me. In the unseen world described by a poet whom M. le Maire has probably heard of, the man who traverses Purgatory (to speak of no other place) is seen by all, and is a wonder to all he meets—his shadow, his breath separate him from those around him. But whether the unseen life has changed, or if it is I who am not worthy their attention, this I know that I stood in our city like a ghost, and no one took any heed of me. When there came back upon me slowly my old desire to inquire, to understand, I was met with this difficulty at the first—that no one heeded me. I went through and through the streets, sometimes I paused to look round, to implore that which swept by me to make itself known. But the stream went along like soft air, like the flowing of a river, setting me aside from time to time, as the air will displace a straw, or the water a stone, but no more. There was neither languor nor lingering. I was the only passive thing, the being without occupation. Would you have paused in your labours to tell an idle traveller the meaning of our lives, before the day when you left Semur? Nor would they: I was driven hither and thither by the current of that life, but no one stepped forth out of the unseen to hear my questions or to answer me how this might be.

You have been made to believe that all was darkness in Semur. M. le Maire, it was not so. The darkness wrapped the walls as in a winding sheet; but within, soon after you were gone, there arose a sweet and wonderful light—a light that was neither of the sun nor of the moon; and presently, after the ringing of the bells; the silence departed as the darkness had departed. I began to hear, first a murmur, then the sound of the going which I had felt without hearing it—then a faint tinkle of voices—and at the last, as my mind grew attuned to these wonders, the very words they said. If they spoke in our language or in another, I cannot tell; but I understood. How long it was before the sensation of their presence was aided by the happiness of hearing I know not, nor do I know how the time has passed, or how long it is, whether years or days, that I have been in Semur with those who are now there; for the light did not vary—there was no night or day. All I know is that suddenly, on awakening from a sleep (for the wonder was that I could sleep, sometimes sitting on the Cathedral steps, sometimes in my own house; where sometimes also I lingered and searched about for the crusts that Leocadie had left), I found the whole world full of sound. They sang going in bands about the streets; they talked to each other as they went along every way. From the houses, all open, where everyone could go who would, there came the soft chiming of those voices. And at first every sound was full of gladness and hope. The song they sang first was like this: 'Send us, send us to our father's house. Many are our brethren, many and dear. They have forgotten, forgotten, forgotten! But when we speak, then will they hear. ' And the others answered: 'We have come, we have come to the house of our fathers. Sweet are the homes, the homes we were born in. As we remember, so will they remember. When we speak, when we speak, they will hear. ' Do not think that these were the words they sang; but it was like this. And as they sang there was joy and expectation everywhere. It was more beautiful than any of our music, for it was full of desire and longing, yet hope and gladness; whereas among us, where there is longing, it is always sad. Later a great singer, I know not who he was, one going past as on a majestic soft wind, sang another song, of which I shall tell you by and by. I do not think he was one of them. They came out to the windows, to the doors, into all the streets and byways to hear him as he went past.

M. le Maire will, however, be good enough to remark that I did not understand all that I heard. In the middle of a phrase, in a word half breathed, a sudden barrier would rise. For a time I laboured after their meaning, trying hard and vainly to understand; but afterwards I perceived that only when they spoke of Semur, of you who were gone forth, and of what was being done, could I make it out. At first this made me only more eager to hear; but when thought came, then

I perceived that of all my longing nothing was satisfied. Though I was alone with the unseen, I comprehended it not; only when it touched upon what I knew, then I understood.

At first all went well. Those who were in the streets, and at the doors and windows of the houses, and on the Cathedral steps, where they seemed to throng, listening to the sounding of the bells, spoke only of this that they had come to do. Of you and you only I heard. They said to each other, with great joy, that the women had been instructed, that they had listened, and were safe. There was pleasure in all the city. The singers were called forth, those who were best instructed (so I judged from what I heard), to take the place of the warders on the walls; and all, as they went along, sang that song: 'Our brothers have forgotten; but when we speak, they will hear. ' How was it, how was it that you did not hear? One time I was by the river porte in a boat; and this song came to me from the walls as sweet as Heaven. Never have I heard such a song. The music was beseeching, it moved the very heart. 'We have come out of the unseen, ' they sang; 'for love of you; believe us, believe us! Love brings us back to earth; believe us, believe us! ' How was it that you did not hear? When I heard those singers sing, I wept; they beguiled the heart out of my bosom. They sang, they shouted, the music swept about all the walls: 'Love brings us back to earth, believe us! ' M. le Maire, I saw you from the river gate; there was a look of perplexity upon your face; and one put his curved hand to his ear as if to listen to some thin far-off sound, when it was like a storm, like a tempest of music!

After that there was a great change in the city. The choirs came back from the walls marching more slowly, and with a sighing through all the air. A sigh, nay, something like a sob breathed through the streets. 'They cannot hear us, or they will not hear us. ' Wherever I turned, this was what I heard: 'They cannot hear us. ' The whole town, and all the houses that were teeming with souls, and all the street, where so many were coming and going was full of wonder and dismay. (If you will take my opinion, they know pain as well as joy, M. le Maire, Those who are in Semur. They are not as gods, perfect and sufficing to themselves, nor are they all-knowing and all-wise, like the good God. They hope like us, and desire, and are mistaken; but do no wrong. This is my opinion. I am no more than other men, that you should accept it without support; but I have lived among them, and this is what I think.) They were taken by surprise; they did not understand it any more than we understand when we have put forth all our strength and fail. They were confounded, if I could judge rightly. Then there arose cries from one to another: 'Do you forget what was said to us? ' and, 'We were warned, we were warned. ' There went a sighing over all the city: 'They cannot hear us, our voices are not as their voices; they cannot see us. We have taken their homes from them, and they know not the reason. ' My heart was wrung for their disappointment. I longed to tell them that neither had I heard at once; but it was only after a time that I ventured upon this. And whether I spoke, and was heard; or if it was read in my heart, I cannot tell. There was a pause made round me as if of wondering and listening, and then, in a moment, in the twinkling of an eye, a face suddenly turned and looked into my face.

M. le Maire, it was the face of your father, Martin Dupin, whom I remember as well as I remember my own father. He was the best man I ever knew. It appeared to me for a moment, that face alone, looking at me with questioning eyes.

There seemed to be agitation and doubt for a time after this; some went out (so I understood) on embassies among you, but could get no hearing; some through the gates, some by the river. And the bells were rung that you might hear and know; but neither could you understand the bells. I wandered from one place to another, listening and watching—till the unseen became to me as the seen, and I thought of the wonder no more. Sometimes there came to me vaguely a desire to question them, to ask whence they came and what was the secret of their living, and why they were here? But if I had asked who would have heard me? and desire had grown faint in my heart; all I wished for was that you should hear, that you should understand; with this wish Semur was full. They thought but of this. They went to the walls in bands, each in their order, and as they came all the others rushed to meet them, to ask, 'What news? ' I following, now with one, now with another, breathless and footsore as they glided along. It is terrible when flesh and blood live with those who are spirits. I toiled after them. I sat on the Cathedral steps, and slept and waked, and heard the voices still in my dream. I prayed, but it was hard to pray. Once following a crowd I entered your house, M. le Maire, and went up, though I scarcely could drag myself along. There many were assembled as in council. Your father was at the head of all. He was the one, he only, who knew me. Again he looked at me and I saw him, and in the light of his face an assembly such as I have seen in pictures. One moment it glimmered before me and then it was gone. There were the captains of all the bands waiting to speak, men and women. I heard them repeating from one to another the same tale. One voice was small and soft like a child's; it spoke of you. 'We went to him, ' it said; and your father, M. le Maire, he too joined in, and said: 'We went to him—but he could not hear us. ' And some said it was enough—that they had no commission from on high, that they were but permitted—that it was their own will to do it—and that the time had come to forbear.

Now, while I listened, my heart was grieved that they should fail. This gave me a wound for myself who had trusted in them, and also for them. But I, who am I, a poor man without credit among my neighbours, a dreamer, one whom many despise, that I should come to their aid? Yet I could not listen and take no part. I cried out: 'Send me. I will tell them in words they understand. ' The sound of my voice was like a roar in that atmosphere. It sent a tremble into the air. It seemed to rend me as it came forth from me, and made me giddy, so that I would have fallen had not there been a support afforded me. As the light was going out of my eyes I saw again the faces looking at each other, questioning, benign, beautiful heads one over another, eyes that were clear as the heavens, but sad. I trembled while I gazed: there was the bliss of heaven in their faces, yet they were sad. Then everything faded. I was led away, I know not how, and brought to the door and put forth. I was not worthy to see the blessed grieve. That is a sight upon which the angels look with awe, and which brings those tears which are salvation into the eyes of God.

I went back to my house, weary yet calm. There were many in my house; but because my heart was full of one who was not there, I knew not those who were there. I sat me down where she had been. I was weary, more weary than ever before, but calm. Then I bethought me that I knew no more than at the first, that I had lived among the unseen as if they were my neighbours, neither fearing them, nor hearing those wonders which they have to tell. As I sat with my head in my hands, two talked to each other close by: 'Is it true that we have failed? ' said one; and the other answered, 'Must not all fail that is not sent of the Father? ' I was silent; but I knew them, they were the voices of my father and my mother. I listened as out of a faint, in a dream.

While I sat thus, with these voices in my ears, which a little while before would have seemed to me more worthy of note than anything on earth, but which now lulled me and comforted me, as a child is comforted by the voices of its guardians in the night, there occurred a new thing in the city like nothing I had heard before. It roused me notwithstanding my exhaustion and stupor. It was the sound as of some one passing through the city suddenly and swiftly, whether in some wonderful chariot, whether on some sweeping mighty wind, I cannot tell. The voices stopped that were conversing beside me, and I stood up, and with an impulse I could not resist went out, as if a king were passing that way. Straight, without turning to the right or left, through the city, from one gate to another, this passenger seemed going; and as he went there was the sound as of a proclamation, as if it were a herald denouncing war or ratifying peace. Whosoever he was, the sweep of his going moved my hair like a wind. At first the proclamation was but as a great shout, and I could not understand it; but as he came nearer the words became distinct. 'Neither will they believe—though one rose from the dead.' As it passed a murmur went up from the city, like the voice of a great multitude. Then there came sudden silence.

At this moment, for a time—M. le Maire will take my statement for what it is worth—I became unconscious of what passed further. Whether weariness overpowered me and I slept, as at the most terrible moment nature will demand to do, or if I fainted I cannot tell; but for a time I knew no more. When I came to myself, I was seated on the Cathedral steps with everything silent around me. From thence I rose up, moved by a will which was not mine, and was led softly across the Grande Rue, through the great square, with my face towards the Porte St. Lambert. I went steadily on without hesitation, never doubting that the gates would open to me, doubting nothing, though I had never attempted to withdraw from the city before. When I came to the gate I said not a word, nor any one to me; but the door rolled slowly open before me, and I was put forth into the morning light, into the shining of the sun. I have now said everything I had to say. The message I delivered was said through me, I can tell no more. Let me rest a little; figure to yourselves, I have known no night of rest, nor eaten a morsel of bread for—did you say it was but three days?

M. LE MAIRE RESUMES HIS NARRATIVE.

We re-entered by the door for foot-passengers which is by the side of the great Porte St. Lambert.

I will not deny that my heart was, as one may say, in my throat. A man does what is his duty, what his fellow-citizens expect of him; but that is not to say that he renders himself callous to natural emotion. My veins were swollen, the blood coursing through them like a high-flowing river; my tongue was parched and dry. I am not ashamed to admit that from head to foot my body quivered and trembled. I was afraid—but I went forward; no man can do more. As for M. le Curé he said not a word. If he had any fears he concealed them as I did. But his occupation is with the ghostly and spiritual. To see men die, to accompany them to the verge of the grave, to create for them during the time of their suffering after death (if it is true that they suffer), an interest in heaven, this his profession must necessarily give him courage. My position is very different. I have not made up my mind upon these subjects. When one can believe frankly in all the Church says, many things become simple, which otherwise cause great difficulty in the mind. The mysterious and wonderful then find their natural place in the course of affairs; but when a man thinks for himself, and has to take everything on his own responsibility, and make all the necessary explanations, there is often great difficulty. So many things will not fit into their places, they straggle like weary men on a march. One cannot put them together, or satisfy one's self.

The sun was shining outside the walls when we re-entered Semur; but the first step we took was into a gloom as black as night, which did not re-assure us, it is unnecessary to say. A chill was in the air, of night and mist. We shivered, not with the nerves only but with the cold. And as all was dark, so all was still. I had expected to feel the presence of those who were there, as I had felt the crowd of the invisible before they entered the city. But the air was vacant, there was nothing but darkness and cold. We went on for a little way with a strange fervour of expectation. At each moment, at each step, it seemed to me that some great call must be made upon my self-possession and courage, some event happen; but there was nothing. All was calm, the houses on either side of the way were open, all but the office of the *octroi* which was black as night with its closed door. M. le Curé has told me since that he believed Them to be there, though unseen. This idea, however, was not in my mind. I had felt the unseen multitude; but here the air was free, there was no one interposing between us, who breathed as men, and the walls that surrounded us. Just within the gate a lamp was burning, hanging to its rope over our heads; and the lights were in the houses as if some one had left them there; they threw a strange glimmer into the darkness, flickering in the wind. By and by as we went on the gloom lessened, and by the time we had reached the Grande Rue, there was a clear steady pale twilight by which we saw everything, as by the light of day.

We stood at the corner of the square and looked round. Although still I heard the beating of my own pulses loudly working in my ears, yet it was less terrible than at first. A city when asleep is wonderful to look on, but in all the closed doors and windows one feels the safety and repose sheltered there which no man can disturb; and the air has in it a sense of life, subdued, yet warm. But here all was open, and all deserted. The house of the miser Grosgain was exposed from the highest to the lowest, but nobody was there to search for what was hidden. The hotel de Bois-Sombre, with its great *porte-cochère,* always so jealously closed; and my own house, which my mother and wife have always guarded so carefully, that no damp nor breath of night might enter, had every door and window wide open. Desolation seemed seated in all these empty places. I feared to go into my own dwelling. It seemed to me as if the dead must be lying within. *Bon Dieu!* Not a soul, not a shadow; all vacant in this soft twilight; nothing moving, nothing visible. The great doors of the Cathedral were wide open, and every little entry. How spacious the city looked, how silent, how wonderful! There was room for a squadron to wheel in the great square, but not so much as a bird, not a dog; all pale and empty. We stood for a long time (or it seemed a long time) at the corner, looking right and left. We were afraid to make a step farther. We knew not what to do. Nor could I speak; there was much I wished to say, but something stopped my voice.

At last M. le Curé found utterance. His voice so moved the silence, that at first my heart was faint with fear; it was hoarse, and the sound rolled round the great square like muffled thunder. One did not seem to know what strange faces might rise at the open windows, what terrors might appear. But all he said was, 'We are ambassadors in vain. '

What was it that followed? My teeth chattered. I could not hear. It was as if 'in vain! —in vain! ' came back in echoes, more and more distant from every opening. They breathed all around us, then were still, then returned louder from beyond the river. M. le Curé, though he is a spiritual person, was no more courageous than I. With one impulse, we put out our hands and grasped each other. We retreated back to back, like men hemmed in by foes, and I felt his heart beating wildly, and he mine. Then silence, silence settled all around.

It was now my turn to speak. I would not be behind, come what might, though my lips were parched with mental trouble.

I said, 'Are we indeed too late? Lecamus must have deceived himself. '

To this there came no echo and no reply, which would be a relief, you may suppose; but it was not so. It was well-nigh more appalling, more terrible than the sound; for though we spoke thus, we did not believe the place was empty. Those whom we approached seemed to be wrapping themselves in silence, invisible, waiting to speak with some awful purpose when their time came.

There we stood for some minutes, like two children, holding each other's hands, leaning against each other at the corner of the square—as helpless as children, waiting for what should come next. I say it frankly, my brain and my heart were one throb. They plunged and beat so wildly that I could scarcely have heard any other sound. In this respect I think he was more calm. There was on his face that look of intense listening which strains the very soul. But neither he nor I heard anything, not so much as a whisper. At last, 'Let us go on, ' I said. We stumbled as we went, with agitation and fear. We were afraid to turn our backs to those empty houses, which seemed to gaze at us with all their empty windows pale and glaring. Mechanically, scarce knowing what I was doing, I made towards my own house.

There was no one there. The rooms were all open and empty. I went from one to another, with a sense of expectation which made my heart faint; but no one was there, nor anything changed. Yet I do wrong to say that nothing was changed. In my library, where I keep my books, where my father and grandfather conducted their affairs, like me, one little difference struck me suddenly, as if some one had dealt me a blow. The old bureau which my grandfather had used, at which I remember standing by his knee, had been drawn from the corner where I had placed it out of the way (to make room for the furniture I preferred), and replaced, as in old times, in the middle of the room. It was nothing; yet how much was in this! though only myself could have perceived it. Some of the old drawers were open, full of old papers. I glanced over there in my agitation, to see if there might be any writing, any message addressed to me; but there was nothing, nothing but this silent sign of those who had been here. Naturally M. le Curé, who kept watch at the door, was unacquainted with the cause of my emotion. The last room I entered was my wife's. Her veil was lying on the white bed, as if she had gone out that moment, and some of her ornaments were on the table. It seemed to me that the atmosphere of mystery which filled the rest of the house was not here. A ribbon, a little ring, what nothings are these? Yet they make even emptiness sweet. In my Agnès's room there is a little shrine, more sacred to us than any altar. There is the picture of our little Marie. It is covered with a veil, embroidered with needlework which it is a wonder to see. Not always can even Agnès bear to look upon the face of this angel, whom God has taken from her. She has worked the little curtain with lilies, with white and virginal flowers; and no hand, not even mine, ever draws it aside. What did I see? The veil was boldly folded away; the face of the child looked at me across her mother's bed, and upon the frame of the picture was laid a branch of olive, with silvery leaves. I know no more but that I uttered a great cry, and flung myself upon my knees before this angel-gift. What stranger could know what was in my heart? M. le Curé, my friend, my brother, came hastily to me, with a pale countenance; but when he looked at me, he drew back and turned away his face, and a sob came from his breast. Never child had called him father, were it in heaven, were it on earth. Well I knew whose tender fingers had placed the branch of olive there.

I went out of the room and locked the door. It was just that my wife should find it where it had been laid.

I put my arm into his as we went out once more into the street. That moment had made us brother and brother. And this union made us more strong. Besides, the silence and the emptiness began to grow less terrible to us. We spoke in our natural voices as we came out, scarcely knowing how great was the difference between them and the whispers which had been all we dared at first to employ. Yet the sound of these louder tones scared us when we heard them, for we were still trembling, not assured of deliverance. It was he who showed himself a man, not I; for my heart was overwhelmed, the tears stood in my eyes, I had no strength to resist my impressions.

'Martin Dupin, ' he said suddenly, 'it is enough. We are frightening ourselves with shadows. We are afraid even of our own voices. This must not be. Enough! Whosoever they were who have been in Semur, their visitation is over, and they are gone. '

'I think so, ' I said faintly; 'but God knows. ' Just then something passed me as sure as ever man passed me. I started back out of the way and dropped my friend's arm, and covered my eyes with my hands. It was nothing that could be seen; it was an air, a breath. M. le Curé looked at me wildly; he was as a man beside himself. He struck his foot upon the pavement and gave a loud and bitter cry.

'Is it delusion? ' he said, 'O my God! or shall not even this, not even so much as this be revealed to me? '

To see a man who had so ruled himself, who had resisted every disturbance and stood fast when all gave way, moved thus at the very last to cry out with passion against that which had been denied to him, brought me back to myself. How often had I read it in his eyes before! He—the priest—the servant of the unseen—yet to all of us lay persons had that been revealed which was hid from him. A great pity was within me, and gave me strength. 'Brother, ' I said, 'we are weak. If we saw heaven opened, could we trust to our vision now? Our imaginations are masters of us. So far as mortal eye can see, we are alone in Semur. Have you forgotten your psalm, and how you sustained us at the first? And now, your Cathedral is open to you, my brother. *Lætatus sum,* ' I said. It was an inspiration from above, and no thought of mine; for it is well known, that though deeply respectful, I have never professed religion. With one impulse we turned, we went together, as in a procession, across the silent place, and up the great steps. We said not a word to each other of what we meant to do. All was fair and silent in the holy place; a breath of incense still in the air; a murmur of psalms (as one could imagine) far up in the high roof. There I served, while he said his mass. It was for my friend that this impulse came to my mind; but I was rewarded. The days of my childhood seemed to come back to me. All trouble, and care, and mystery, and pain, seemed left behind. All I could see was the glimmer on the altar of the great candle-sticks, the sacred pyx in its shrine, the chalice, and the book. I was again an *enfant de choeur* robed in white, like the angels, no doubt, no disquiet in my soul—and my father kneeling behind among the faithful, bowing his head, with a sweetness which I too knew, being a father, because it was his child that tinkled the bell and swung the censer. Never since those days have I served the mass. My heart grew soft within me as the heart of a little child. The voice of M. le Curé was full of tears—it swelled out into the air and filled the vacant place. I knelt behind him on the steps of the altar and wept.

Then there came a sound that made our hearts leap in our bosoms. His voice wavered as if it had been struck by a strong wind; but he was a brave man, and he went on. It was the bells of the Cathedral that pealed out over our heads. In the midst of the office, while we knelt all alone, they began to ring as at Easter or some great festival. At first softly, almost sadly, like choirs of distant singers, that died away and were echoed and died again; then taking up another strain, they rang out into the sky with hurrying notes and clang of joy. The effect upon myself was wonderful. I no longer felt any fear. The illusion was complete. I was a child again, serving the mass in my little surplice—aware that all who loved me were kneeling behind, that the good God was smiling, and the Cathedral bells ringing out their majestic Amen.

M. le Curé came down the altar steps when his mass was ended. Together we put away the vestments and the holy vessels. Our hearts were soft; the weight was taken from them. As we came out the bells were dying away in long and low echoes, now faint, now louder, like mingled voices of gladness and regret. And whereas it had been a pale twilight when we entered, the clearness of the day had rolled sweetly in, and now it was fair morning in all the streets. We did not say a word to each other, but arm and arm took our way to the gates, to open to our neighbours, to call all our fellow-citizens back to Semur.

If I record here an incident of another kind, it is because of the sequel that followed. As we passed by the hospital of St. Jean, we heard distinctly, coming from within, the accents of a feeble yet impatient voice. The sound revived for a moment the troubles that were stilled within us—but only for a moment. This was no visionary voice. It brought a smile to the grave face of M. le Curé and tempted me well nigh to laughter, so strangely did this sensation of the actual, break and disperse the visionary atmosphere. We went in without any timidity, with a conscious relaxation of the great strain upon us. In a little nook, curtained off from the great ward, lay a sick man upon his bed. 'Is it M. le Maire? ' he said; 'à la bonne heure! I have a complaint to make of the nurses for the night. They have gone out to amuse themselves; they take no notice of poor sick people. They have known for a week that I could not sleep; but neither have they given me a sleeping draught, nor endeavoured to distract me with cheerful conversation. And to-day, look you, M. le Maire, not one of the sisters has come near me! '

'Have you suffered, my poor fellow? ' I said; but he would not go so far as this.

'I don't want to make complaints, M. le Maire; but the sisters do not come themselves as they used to do. One does not care to have a strange nurse, when one knows that if the sisters did their duty—But if it does not occur any more I do not wish it to be thought that I am the one to complain. '

'Do not fear, mon ami, ' I said. 'I will say to the Reverend Mother that you have been left too long alone. '

'And listen, M. le Maire, ' cried the man; 'those bells, will they never be done? My head aches with the din they make. How can one go to sleep with all that riot in one's ears? '

We looked at each other, we could not but smile. So that which is joy and deliverance to one is vexation to another. As we went out again into the street the lingering music of the bells died out, and (for the first time for all these terrible days and nights) the great clock struck the hour. And as the clock struck, the last cloud rose like a mist and disappeared in flying vapours, and the full sunshine of noon burst on Semur.

SUPPLEMENT BY M. DE BOIS-SOMBRE.

When M. le Maire disappeared within the mist, we all remained behind with troubled hearts. For my own part I was alarmed for my friend. M. Martin Dupin is not noble. He belongs, indeed, to the *haute bourgeoisie,* and all his antecedents are most respectable; but it is his personal character and admirable qualities which justify me in calling him my friend. The manner in which he has performed his duties to his fellow-citizens during this time of distress has been sublime. It is not my habit to take any share in public life; the unhappy circumstances of France have made this impossible for years. Nevertheless, I put aside my scruples when it became necessary, to leave him free for his mission. I gave no opinion upon that mission itself, or how far he was right in obeying the advice of a hare-brained enthusiast like Lecamus. Nevertheless the moment had come at which our banishment had become intolerable. Another day, and I should have proposed an assault upon the place. Our dead forefathers, though I would speak of them with every respect, should not presume upon their privilege. I do not pretend to be braver than other men, nor have I shown myself more equal than others to cope with the present emergency. But I have the impatience of my countrymen, and rather than rot here outside the gates, parted from Madame de Bois-Sombre and my children, who, I am happy to state, are in safety at the country house of the brave Dupin, I should have dared any hazard. This being the case, a new step of any kind called for my approbation, and I could not refuse under the circumstances—especially as no ceremony of installation was required or profession of loyalty to one government or another—to take upon me the office of coadjutor and act as deputy for my friend Martin outside the walls of Semur.

The moment at which I assumed the authority was one of great discouragement and depression. The men were tired to death. Their minds were worn out as well as their bodies. The excitement and fatigue had been more than they could bear. Some were for giving up the contest and seeking new homes for themselves. These were they, I need not remark, who had but little to lose; some seemed to care for nothing but to lie down and rest. Though it produced a great movement among us when Lecamus suddenly appeared coming out of the city; and the undertaking of Dupin and the excellent Curé was viewed with great interest, yet there could not but be signs apparent that the situation had lasted too long. It was *tendu* in the strongest degree, and when that is the case a reaction must come. It is impossible to say, for one thing, how treat was our personal discomfort. We were as soldiers campaigning without a commissariat, or any precautions taken for our welfare; no food save what was sent to us from La Clairière and other places; no means of caring for our personal appearance, in which lies so much of the materials of self respect. I say nothing of the chief features of all—the occupation of our homes by others—the forcible expulsion of which we had been the objects. No one could have been more deeply impressed than myself at the moment of these extraordinary proceedings; but we cannot go on with one monotonous impression, however serious, we other Frenchmen. Three days is a very long time to dwell in one thought; I myself had become impatient, I do not deny. To go away, which would have been very natural, and which Agathe proposed, was contrary to my instincts and interests both. I trust I can obey the logic of circumstances as well as another; but to yield is not easy, and to leave my hotel at Semur—now the chief residence, alas! of the Bois-Sombres—probably to the licence of a mob—for one can never tell at what moment Republican institutions may break down and sink back into the chaos from which they arose—was impossible. Nor would I forsake the brave Dupin without the strongest motive; but that the situation was extremely *tendu,* and a reaction close at hand, was beyond dispute.

I resisted the movement which my excellent friend made to take off and transfer to me his scarf of office. These things are much thought of among the *bourgeoisie. 'Mon ami,* ' I said, 'you cannot tell what use you may have for it; whereas our townsmen know me, and that I am not one to take up an unwarrantable position. ' We then accompanied him to the neighbourhood of the Porte St. Lambert. It was at that time invisible; we could but judge approximately. My men were unwilling to approach too near, neither did I myself think it necessary. We parted, after giving the two envoys an honourable escort, leaving a clear space between us and the darkness. To see them disappear gave us all a startling sensation. Up to the last moment I had doubted whether they would obtain admittance. When they disappeared from our eyes, there came upon all of us an impulse of alarm. I myself was so far moved by it, that I called out after them in a sudden panic. For if any catastrophe had happened, how could I ever have forgiven myself, especially as Madame Dupin de la Clairière, a person entirely *comme il faut,* and of the most distinguished character, went after her husband, with a touching devotion, following him to the very edge of the darkness? I do not think, so deeply possessed was he by his mission, that he saw her. Dupin is very determined in his way; but he is imaginative and thoughtful, and it is very possible that, as he required all his powers to brace him for this enterprise, he made it a principle neither to look to the right hand nor the left. When we paused, and following after our two representatives, Madame Dupin stepped forth, a thrill ran through us all. Some would have called to her, for I heard many broken exclamations; but most of us were too much startled to speak. We thought nothing less than that she was about to risk herself by going after them into the city. If that was her intention—and nothing is more probable; for women are very daring, though they are timid—she was stopped, it is most likely, by that curious inability to move a step farther which we have all experienced. We saw her pause, clasp her hands in despair (or it might be in token of farewell to her husband), then, instead of returning, seat herself on the road on the edge of the darkness. It was a relief to all who were looking on to see her there.

In the reaction after that excitement I found myself in face of a great difficulty—what to do with my men, to keep them from demoralisation. They were greatly excited; and yet there was nothing to be done for them, for myself, for any of us, but to wait. To organise the patrol again, under the circumstances, would have been impossible. Dupin, perhaps, might have tried it with that *bourgeois* determination which so often carries its point in spite of all higher intelligence; but to me, who have not this commonplace way of looking at things, it was impossible. The worthy soul did not think in what a difficulty he left us. That intolerable, good-for-nothing Jacques Richard (whom Dupin protects unwisely, I cannot tell why), and who was already half-seas-over, had drawn several of his comrades with him towards the *cabaret*, which was always a danger to us. 'We will drink success to M. le Maire, ' he said, '*mes bons amis*! That can do no one any harm; and as we have spoken up, as we have empowered him to offer handsome terms to *Messieurs les Morts*——'

It was intolerable. Precisely at the moment when our fortune hung in the balance, and when, perhaps, an indiscreet word—'Arrest that fellow, ' I said. 'Riou, you are an official; you understand your duty. Arrest him on the spot, and confine him in the tent out of the way of mischief. Two of you mount guard over him. And let a party be told off, of which you will take the command, Louis Bertin, to go at once to La Clairière and beg the Reverend Mothers of the hospital to favour us with their presence. It will be well to have those excellent ladies in our front whatever happens; and you may communicate to them the unanimous decision about their chapel. You, Robert Lemaire, with an escort, will proceed to the *campagne* of M. Barbou, and put him in possession of the circumstances. Those of you who have a natural wish to seek a little repose will consider yourselves as discharged from duty and permitted to do so. Your Maire having confided to me his authority—not without your consent—(this I avow I added with some difficulty, for who cared for their assent? but a Republican Government offers a premium to every insincerity), I wait with confidence to see these dispositions carried out. '

This, I am happy to say, produced the best effect. They obeyed me without hesitation; and, fortunately for me, slumber seized upon the majority. Had it not been for this, I can scarcely tell how I should have got out of it. I felt drowsy myself, having been with the patrol the greater part of the night; but to yield to such weakness was, in my position, of course impossible.

This, then, was our attitude during the last hours of suspense, which were perhaps the most trying of all. In the distance might be seen the little bands marching towards La Clairière, on one side, and M. Barbou's country-house ('La Corbeille des Raisins') on the other. It goes without saying that I did not want M. Barbou, but it was the first errand I could think of. Towards the city, just where the darkness began that enveloped it, sat Madame Dupin. That *sainte femme* was praying for her husband, who could doubt? And under the trees, wherever they could find a favourable spot, my men lay down on the grass, and most of them fell asleep. My eyes were heavy enough, but responsibility drives away rest. I had but one nap of five minutes' duration, leaning against a tree, when it occurred to me that Jacques Richard, whom I sent under escort half-drunk to the tent, was not the most admirable companion for that poor visionary Lecamus, who had been accommodated there. I roused myself, therefore, though unwillingly, to see whether these two, so discordant, could agree.

I met Lecamus at the tent-door. He was coming out, very feeble and tottering, with that dazed look which (according to me) has always been characteristic of him. He had a bundle of papers in his hand. He had been setting in order his report of what had happened to him, to be submitted to the Maire. 'Monsieur, ' he said, with some irritation (which I forgave him), 'you have always been unfavourable to me. I owe it to you that this unhappy drunkard has been sent to disturb me in my feebleness and the discharge of a public duty. '

'My good Monsieur Lecamus, ' said I, 'you do my recollection too much honour. The fact is, I had forgotten all about you and your public duty. Accept my excuses. Though indeed your supposition that I should have taken the trouble to annoy you, and your description of that good-for-nothing as an unhappy drunkard, are signs of intolerance which I should not have expected in a man so favoured. '

This speech, though too long, pleased me, for a man of this species, a revolutionary (are not all visionaries revolutionaries?) is always, when occasion offers, to be put down. He disarmed me, however, by his humility. He gave a look round. 'Where can I go? ' he said, and there was pathos in his voice. At length he perceived Madame Dupin sitting almost motionless on the road. 'Ah! ' he said, 'there is my place. ' The man, I could not but perceive, was very weak. His eyes were twice their natural size, his face was the colour of ashes; through his whole frame there was a trembling; the papers shook in his hand. A compunction seized my mind: I regretted to have sent that piece of noise and folly to disturb a poor man so suffering and weak. 'Monsieur Lecamus, ' I said, 'forgive me. I acknowledge that it was inconsiderate. Remain here in comfort, and I will find for this unruly fellow another place of confinement. '

'Nay, ' he said, 'there is my place, ' pointing to where Madame Dupin sat. I felt disposed for a moment to indulge in a pleasantry, to say that I approved his taste; but on second thoughts I forebore. He went tottering slowly across the broken ground, hardly able to drag himself along. 'Has he had any refreshment? ' I asked of one of the women who were about. They told me yes, and this restored my composure; for after all I had not meant to annoy him, I had forgotten he was there—a trivial fault in circumstances so exciting. I was more easy in my mind, however, I confess it, when I saw that he had reached his chosen position safely. The man looked so weak. It seemed to me that he might have died on the road.

I thought I could almost perceive the gate, with Madame Dupin seated under the battlements, her charming figure relieved against the gloom, and that poor Lecamus lying, with his papers fluttering at her feet. This was the last thing I was conscious of.

EXTRACT FROM THE NARRATIVE OF MADAME DUPIN DE LA CLAIRIÈRE (*née* DE CHAMPFLEURIE).

I went with my husband to the city gate. I did not wish to distract his mind from what he had undertaken, therefore I took care he should not see me; but to follow close, giving the sympathy of your whole heart, must not that be a support? If I am asked whether I was content to let him go, I cannot answer yes; but had another than Martin been chosen, I could not have borne it. What I desired, was to go myself. I was not afraid: and if it had proved dangerous, if I had been broken and crushed to pieces between the seen and the unseen, one could not have had a more beautiful fate. It would have made me happy to go. But perhaps it was better that the messenger should not be a woman; they might have said it was delusion, an attack of the nerves. We are not trusted in these respects, though I find it hard to tell why.

But I went with Martin to the gate. To go as far as was possible, to be as near as possible, that was something. If there had been room for me to pass, I should have gone, and with such gladness! for God He knows that to help to thrust my husband into danger, and not to share it, was terrible to me. But no; the invisible line was still drawn, beyond which I could not stir. The door opened before him, and closed upon me. But though to see him disappear into the gloom was anguish, yet to know that he was the man by whom the city should be saved was sweet. I sat down on the spot where my steps were stayed. It was close to the wall, where there is a ledge of stonework round the basement of the tower. There I sat down to wait till he should come again.

If any one thinks, however, that we, who were under the shelter of the roof of La Clairière were less tried than our husbands, it is a mistake; our chief grief was that we were parted from them, not knowing what suffering, what exposure they might have to bear, and knowing that they would not accept, as most of us were willing to accept, the interpretation of the mystery; but there was a certain comfort in the fact that we had to be very busy, preparing a little food to take to them, and feeding the others. La Clairière is a little country house, not a great château, and it was taxed to the utmost to afford some covert to the people. The children were all sheltered and cared for; but as for the rest of us we did as we could. And how gay they were, all the little ones! What was it to them all that had happened? It was a fête for them to be in the country, to be so many together, to run in the fields and the gardens. Sometimes their laughter and their happiness were more than we could bear. Agathe de Bois-Sombre, who takes life hardly, who is more easily deranged than I, was one who was much disturbed by this. But was it not to preserve the children that we were commanded to go to La Clairière? Some of the women also were not easy to bear with. When they were put into our rooms they too found it a fête, and sat down among the children, and ate and drank, and forgot what it was; what awful reason had driven us out of our homes. These were not, oh let no one think so! the majority; but there were some, it cannot be denied; and it was difficult for me to calm down Bonne Maman, and keep her from sending them away with their babes. 'But they are *misérables,* ' she said. 'If they were to wander and be lost, if they were to suffer as thou sayest, where would be the harm? I have no patience with the idle, with those who impose upon thee. ' It is possible that Bonne Maman was right—but what then? 'Preserve the children and the sick, ' was the mission that had been given to me. My own room was made the hospital. Nor did this please Bonne Maman. She bid me if I did not stay in it myself to give it to the Bois-Sombres, to some who deserved it. But is it not they who need most who deserve most? Bonne Maman cannot bear that the poor and wretched should live in her Martin's chamber. He is my Martin no less. But to give it up to our Lord is not that to sanctify it? There are who have put Him into their own bed when they imagined they were but sheltering a sick beggar there; that He should have the best was sweet to me: and could not I pray all the better that our Martin should be enlightened, should come to the true sanctuary? When I said this Bonne Maman wept. It was the grief of her heart that Martin thought otherwise than as we do. Nevertheless she said, 'He is so good; the *bon Dieu* knows how good he is; ' as if even his mother could know that so well as I!

But with the women and the children crowding everywhere, the sick in my chamber, the helpless in every corner, it will be seen that we, too, had much to do. And our hearts were elsewhere, with those who were watching the city, who were face to face with those in whom they had not believed. We were going and coming all day long with food for them, and there never was a time of the night or day that there were not many of us watching on the brow of the hill to see if any change came in Semur. Agathe and I, and our children, were all together in one little room. She believed in God, but it was not any comfort to her; sometimes she would weep and pray all day long;

sometimes entreat her husband to abandon the city, to go elsewhere and live, and fly from this strange fate. She is one who cannot endure to be unhappy—not to have what she wishes. As for me, I was brought up in poverty, and it is no wonder if I can more easily submit. She was not willing that I should come this morning to Semur. In the night the Mère Julie had roused us, saying she had seen a procession of angels coming to restore us to the city. Ah! to those who have no knowledge it is easy to speak of processions of angels. But to those who have seen what an angel is—how they flock upon us unawares in the darkness, so that one is confused, and scarce can tell if it is reality or a dream; to those who have heard a little voice soft as the dew coming out of heaven! I said to them—for all were in a great tumult—that the angels do not come in processions, they steal upon us unaware, they reveal themselves in the soul. But they did not listen to me; even Agathe took pleasure in hearing of the revelation. As for me, I had denied myself, I had not seen Martin for a night and a day. I took one of the great baskets, and I went with the women who were the messengers for the day. A purpose formed itself in my heart, it was to make my way into the city, I know not how, and implore them to have pity upon us before the people were distraught. Perhaps, had I been able to refrain from speaking to Martin, I might have found the occasion I wished; but how could I conceal my desire from my husband? And now all is changed, I am rejected and he is gone. He was more worthy. Bonne Maman is right. Our good God, who is our father, does He require that one should make profession of faith, that all should be alike? He sees the heart; and to choose my Martin, does not that prove that He loves best that which is best, not I, or a priest, or one who makes professions? Thus, I sat down at the gate with a great confidence, though also a trembling in my heart. He who had known how to choose him among all the others, would not He guard him? It was a proof to me once again that heaven is true, that the good God loves and comprehends us all, to see how His wisdom, which is unerring, had chosen the best man in Semur.

And M. le Curé, that goes without saying, he is a priest of priests, a true servant of God.

I saw my husband go: perhaps, God knows, into danger, perhaps to some encounter such as might fill the world with awe—to meet those who read the thought in your mind before it comes to your lips. Well! there is no thought in Martin that is not noble and true. Me, I have follies in my heart, every kind of folly; but he! —the tears came in a flood to my eyes, but I would not shed them, as if I were weeping for fear and sorrow—no—but for happiness to know that falsehood was not in him. My little Marie, a holy virgin, may look into her father's heart—I do not fear the test.

The sun came warm to my feet as I sat on the foundation of our city, but the projection of the tower gave me a little shade. All about was a great peace. I thought of the psalm which says, 'He will give it to His beloved sleeping'—that is true; but always there are some who are used as instruments, who are not permitted to sleep. The sounds that came from the people gradually ceased; they were all very quiet. M. de Bois-Sombre I saw at a distance making his dispositions. Then M. Paul Lecamus, whom I had long known, came up across the field, and seated himself close to me upon the road. I have always had a great sympathy with him since the death of his wife; ever since there has been an abstraction in his eyes, a look of desolation. He has no children or any one to bring him back to life. Now, it seemed to me that he had the air of a man who was dying. He had been in the city while all of us had been outside.

'Monsieur Lecamus, ' I said, 'you look very ill, and this is not a place for you. Could not I take you somewhere, where you might be more at your ease? '

'It is true, Madame, ' he said, 'the road is hard, but the sunshine is sweet; and when I have finished what I am writing for M. le Maire, it will be over. There will be no more need—'

I did not understand what he meant. I asked him to let me help him, but he shook his head. His eyes were very hollow, in great caves, and his face was the colour of ashes. Still he smiled. 'I thank you, Madame, ' he said, 'infinitely; everyone knows that Madame Dupin is kind; but when it is done, I shall be free. '

'I am sure, M. Lecamus, that my husband—that M. le Maire—would not wish you to trouble yourself, to be hurried—'

'No, ' he said, 'not he, but I. Who else could write what I have to write? It must be done while it is day. '

'Then there is plenty of time, M. Lecamus. All the best of the day is yet to come; it is still morning. If you could but get as far as La Clairière. There we would nurse you—restore you. '

He shook his head. 'You have enough on your hands at La Clairière,' he said; and then, leaning upon the stones, he began to write again with his pencil. After a time, when he stopped, I ventured to ask—'Monsieur Lecamus, is it, indeed, Those——whom we have known, who are in Semur? '

He turned his dim eyes upon me. 'Does Madame Dupin, ' he said, 'require to ask? '

'No, no. It is true. I have seen and heard. But yet, when a little time passes, you know? one wonders; one asks one's self, was it a dream?'

'That is what I fear, ' he said. 'I, too, if life went on, might ask, notwithstanding all that has occurred to me, Was it a dream? '

'M. Lecamus, you will forgive me if I hurt you. You saw—*her*? '

'No. Seeing—what is seeing? It is but a vulgar sense, it is not all; but I sat at her feet. She was with me. We were one, as of old——. ' A gleam of strange light came into his dim eyes. 'Seeing is not everything, Madame. '

'No, M. Lecamus. I heard the dear voice of my little Marie. '

'Nor is hearing everything, ' he said hastily. 'Neither did she speak; but she was there. We were one; we had no need to speak. What is speaking or hearing when heart wells into heart? For a very little moment, only for a moment, Madame Dupin. '

I put out my hand to him; I could not say a word. How was it possible that she could go away again, and leave him so feeble, so worn, alone?

'Only a very little moment, ' he said, slowly. 'There were other voices—but not hers. I think I am glad it was in the spirit we met, she and I—I prefer not to see her till—after——'

'Oh, M. Lecamus, I am too much of the world! To see them, to hear them—it is for this I long. '

'No, dear Madame. I would not have it till—after——. But I must make haste, I must write, I hear the hum approaching——'

I could not tell what he meant; but I asked no more. How still everything was The people lay asleep on the grass, and I, too, was overwhelmed by the great quiet. I do not know if I slept, but I dreamed. I saw a child very fair and tall always near me, but hiding her face. It appeared to me in my dream that all I wished for was to see this hidden countenance, to know her name; and that I followed and watched her, but for a long time in vain. All at once she turned full upon me, held out her arms to me. Do I need to say who it was? I cried out in my dream to the good God, that He had done well to take her from me—that this was worth it all. Was it a dream? I would not give that dream for rears of waking life. Then I started and came back, in a moment, to the still morning sunshine, the sight of the men asleep, the roughness of the wall against which I leant. Some one laid a hand on mine. I opened my eyes, not knowing what it was—if it might be my husband coming back, or her whom I had seen in my dream. It was M. Lecamus. He had risen up upon his knees—his papers were all laid aside. His eyes in those hollow caves were opened wide, and quivering with a strange light. He had caught my wrist with his worn hand. 'Listen! ' he said; his voice fell to a whisper; a light broke over his face. 'Listen! ' he cried; 'they are coming. ' While he thus grasped my wrist, holding up his weak and wavering body in that strained attitude, the moments passed very slowly. I was afraid of him, of his worn face and thin hands, and the wild eagerness about him. I am ashamed to say it, but so it was. And for this reason it seemed long to me, though I think not more than a minute, till suddenly the bells rang out, sweet and glad as they ring at Easter for the resurrection. There had been ringing of bells before, but not like this. With a start and universal movement the sleeping men got up from where they lay—not one but every one, coming out of the little hollows and from under the trees as if from graves. They all sprang up to listen, with one impulse; and as for me, knowing that Martin was in the city, can it be wondered at if my heart beat so loud that I was incapable of thought of others! What brought me to myself was the strange weight of M. Lecamus on my arm. He put his other hand upon me, all cold in the brightness, all trembling. He raised himself thus slowly to his feet. When I looked at him I shrieked aloud. I forgot all else. His face was transformed—a smile came upon it that was ineffable—the light blazed up, and then quivered and flickered in his eyes like a dying flame. All this time he was leaning his weight upon my arm. Then suddenly he loosed his hold of me, stretched out his hands, stood up, and—died. My God! shall I ever forget him as he stood—his head raised, his hands held out, his lips moving, the eyelids opened wide with a quiver, the light flickering and dying He died first, standing up, saying something with his pale lips—then fell. And it seemed to me all at once, and for a moment, that I heard a sound of many people marching past, the murmur and hum of a great multitude; and softly, softly I was put out of the way, and a voice said, '*Adieu, ma soeur.* ' '*Ma soeur*! ' who called me '*Ma soeur*'? I have no sister. I cried out, saying I know not what. They told me after that I wept and wrung my hands, and said, 'Not thee, not thee, Marie! ' But after that I knew no more.

THE NARRATIVE of MADAME VEUVE DUPIN (*née* LEPELLETIER).

To complete the *procés verbal*, my son wishes me to give my account of the things which happened out of Semur during its miraculous occupation, as it is his desire, in the interests of truth, that nothing should be left out. In this I find a great difficulty for many reasons; in the first place, because I have not the aptitude of expressing myself in writing, and it may well be that the phrases I employ may fail in the correctness which good French requires; and again, because it is my misfortune not to agree in all points with my Martin, though I am proud to think that he is, in every relation of life, so good a man, that the women of his family need not hesitate to follow his advice—but necessarily there are some points which one reserves; and I cannot but feel the closeness of the connection between the late remarkable exhibition of the power of Heaven and the outrage done upon the good Sisters of St. Jean by the administration, of which unfortunately my son is at the head. I say unfortunately, since it is the spirit of independence and pride in him which has resisted all the warnings offered by Divine Providence, and which refuses even now to right the wrongs of the Sisters of St. Jean; though, if it may be permitted to me to say it, as his mother, it was very fortunate in the late troubles that Martin Dupin found himself at the head of the Commune of Semur—since who else could have kept his self-control as he did? —caring for all things and forgetting nothing; who else would, with so much courage, have entered the city? and what other man, being a person of the world and secular in all his thoughts, as, alas! it is so common for men to be, would have so nobly acknowledged his obligations to the good God when our misfortunes were over? My constant prayers for his conversion do not make me incapable of perceiving the nobility of his conduct. When the evidence has been incontestible he has not hesitated to make a public profession of his gratitude, which all will acknowledge to be the sign of a truly noble mind and a heart of gold.

I have long felt that the times were ripe for some exhibition of the power of God. Things have been going very badly among us. Not only have the powers of darkness triumphed over our holy church, in a manner ever to be wept and mourned by all the faithful, and which might have been expected to bring down fire from Heaven upon our heads, but the corruption of popular manners (as might also have been expected) has been daily arising to a pitch unprecedented. The fêtes may indeed be said to be observed, but in what manner? In the cabarets rather than in the churches; and as for the fasts and vigils, who thinks of them? who attends to those sacred moments of penitence? Scarcely even a few ladies are found to do so, instead of the whole population, as in duty bound. I have even seen it happen that my daughter-in-law and myself, and her friend Madame de Bois-Sombre, and old Mère Julie from the market, have formed the whole congregation. Figure to yourself the *bon Dieu* and all the blessed saints looking down from heaven to hear—four persons only in our great Cathedral! I trust that I know that the good God does not despise even two or three; but if any one will think of it—the great bells rung, and the candles lighted, and the curé in his beautiful robes, and all the companies of heaven looking on—and only us four! This shows the neglect of all sacred ordinances that was in Semur. While, on the other hand, what grasping there was for money; what fraud and deceit; what foolishness and dissipation! Even the Mère Julie herself, though a devout person, the pears she sold to us on the last market day before these events, were far, very far, as she must have known, from being satisfactory. In the same way Gros-Jean, though a peasant from our own village near La Clairière, and a man for whom we have often done little services, attempted to impose upon me about the wood for the winter's use, the very night before these occurrences. 'It is enough, ' I cried out, 'to bring the dead out of their graves. ' I did not know—the holy saints forgive me! —how near it was to the moment when this should come true.

And perhaps it is well that I should admit without concealment that I am not one of the women to whom it has been given to see those who came back. There are moments when I will not deny I have asked myself why those others should have been so privileged and never I. Not even in a dream do I see those whom I have lost; yet I think that I too have loved them as well as any have been loved. I have stood by their beds to the last; I have closed their beloved eyes. *Mon Dieu! mon Dieu!* have not I drunk of that cup to the dregs? But never to me, never to me, has it been permitted either to see or to hear. *Bien*! it has been so ordered. Agnès, my daughter-in-law, is a good woman. I have not a word to say against her; and if there are moments when my heart rebels, when I ask myself why she should have her eyes opened and not I, the good God knows that I do not complain against His will—it is in His hand to do as He pleases. And if I receive no privileges, yet have I the privilege which is best, which is, as M. le Curé justly observes, the highest of all— that of doing my duty. In this I thank the good Lord our Seigneur that my Martin has never needed to be ashamed of his mother.

I will also admit that when it was first made apparent to me—not by the sounds of voices which the others heard, but by the use of my reason which I humbly believe is also a gift of God—that the way in which I could best serve both those of the city and my son Martin, who is over them, was to lead the way with the children and all the helpless to La Clairière, thus relieving the watchers, there was for a time a great struggle in my bosom. What were they all to me, that I should desert my Martin, my only son, the child of my old age; he who is as his father, as dear, and yet more dear, because he is his father's son? 'What! (I said in my heart) abandon thee, my child? nay, rather abandon life and every consolation; for what is life to me but thee? ' But while my heart swelled with this cry, suddenly it became apparent to me how many there were holding up their hands helplessly to him, clinging to him so that he could not move. To whom else could they turn? He was the one among all who preserved his courage, who neither feared nor failed. When those voices rang out from the walls—which some understood, but which I did not understand, and many more with me—though my heart was wrung with straining my ears to listen if there was not a voice for me too, yet at the same time this thought was working in my heart. There was a poor woman close to me with little children clinging to her; neither did she know what those voices said. Her eyes turned from Semur, all lost in the darkness, to the sky above us and to me beside her, all confused and bewildered; and the children clung to her, all in tears, crying with that wail which is endless—the trouble of childhood which does not know why it is troubled. 'Maman! Maman! ' they cried, 'let us go home. ' 'Oh! be silent, my little ones, ' said the poor woman; 'be silent; we will go to M. le Maire—he will not leave us without a friend. ' It was then that I saw what my duty was. But it was with a pang—*bon Dieu!* —when I turned my back upon my Martin, when I went away to shelter, to peace, leaving my son thus in face of an offended Heaven and all the invisible powers, do you suppose it was a whole heart I carried in my breast? But no! it was nothing save a great ache—a struggle as of death. But what of that? I had my duty to do, as he had—and as he did not flinch, so did not I; otherwise he would have been ashamed of his mother—and I? I should have felt that the blood was not mine which ran in his veins.

No one can tell what it was, that march to La Clairière. Agnès at first was like an angel. I hope I always do Madame Martin justice. She is a saint. She is good to the bottom of her heart. Nevertheless, with those natures which are enthusiast—which are upborne by excitement—there is also a weakness. Though she was brave as the holy Pucelle when we set out, after a while she flagged like another. The colour went out of her face, and though she smiled still, yet the tears came to her eyes, and she would have wept with the other women, and with the wail of the weary children, and all the agitation, and the weariness, and the length of the way, had not I recalled her to herself. 'Courage! ' I said to her. 'Courage, *ma fille!* We will throw open all the chambers. I will give up even that one in which my Martin Dupin, the father of thy husband, died. ' '*Ma mère,* ' she said, holding my hand to her bosom, 'he is not dead—he is in Semur. ' Forgive me, dear Lord! It gave me a pang that she could see him and not I. 'For me, ' I cried, 'it is enough to know that my good man is in heaven: his room, which I have kept sacred, shall be given up to the poor. ' But oh! the confusion of the stumbling, weary feet; the little children that dropped by the way, and caught at our skirts, and wailed and sobbed; the poor mothers with babes upon each arm, with sick hearts and failing limbs. One cry seemed to rise round us as we went, each infant moving the others to sympathy, till it rose like one breath, a wail of 'Maman! Maman! ' a cry that had no meaning, through having so much meaning. It was difficult not to cry out too in the excitement, in the labouring of the long, long, confused, and tedious way. 'Maman! Maman! ' The Holy Mother could not but hear it. It is not possible but that she must have looked out upon us, and heard us, so helpless as we were, where she sits in heaven.

When we got to La Clairière we were ready to sink down with fatigue like all the rest—nay, even more than the rest, for we were not used to it, and for my part I had altogether lost the habitude of long walks. But then you could see what Madame Martin was. She is slight and fragile and pale, not strong, as any one can perceive; but she rose above the needs of the body. She was the one among us who rested not. We threw open all the rooms, and the poor people thronged in. Old Léontine, who is the *garde* of the house, gazed upon us and the crowd whom we brought with us with great eyes full of fear and trouble. 'But, Madame, ' she cried, 'Madame! ' following me as I went above to the better rooms. She pulled me by my robe. She pushed the poor women with their children away. '*Allez donc, allez*!—rest outside till these ladies have time to speak to you, ' she said; and pulled me by my sleeve. Then 'Madame Martin is putting all this *canaille* into our very chambers, ' she cried. She had always distrusted Madame Martin, who was taken by the peasants for a clerical and a dévote, because she was noble. 'The *bon Dieu* be praised that Madame also is here, who has sense and will regulate everything. ' 'These are no *canaille,* ' I said: 'be silent, *ma bonne* Léontine, here is something which you cannot understand. This is Semur which has come out to us for lodging. ' She let the keys drop out of her hands. It was not wonderful if she was amazed. All day long she followed me about, her very mouth open with wonder. 'Madame Martin, that understands itself, ' she would say. 'She is romanesque—she has imagination—but Madame, Madame has *bon sens*—who would have believed it of Madame? ' Léontine had been my *femme de ménage* long before there was a Madame Martin, when my son was young; and naturally it was of me she still thought. But I cannot put down all the trouble we had ere we found shelter for every one. We filled the stables and the great barn, and all the cottages near; and to get them food, and to have something provided for those who were watching before the city, and who had no one but us to think of them, was a task which was almost beyond our powers. Truly it was beyond our powers—but the Holy Mother of heaven and the good angels helped us. I cannot tell to any one how it was accomplished, yet it was accomplished. The wail of the little ones ceased. They slept that first night as if they had been in heaven. As for us, when the night came, and the dews and the darkness, it seemed to us as if we were out of our bodies, so weary were we, so weary that we could not rest. From La Clairière on ordinary occasions it is a beautiful sight to see the lights of Semur shining in all the high windows, and the streets throwing up a faint whiteness upon the sky; but how strange it was now to look down and see nothing but a darkness—a cloud, which was the city! The lights of the watchers in their camp were invisible to us, —they were so small and low upon the broken ground that we could not see them. Our Agnès crept close to me; we went with one accord to the seat before the door. We did not say 'I will go, ' but went by one impulse, for our hearts were there; and we were glad to taste the freshness of the night and be silent after all our labours. We leant upon each other in our weariness. 'Ma mère, ' she said, 'where is he now, our Martin? ' and wept. 'He is where there is the most to do, be thou sure of that, ' I cried, but wept not. For what did I bring him into the world but for this end?

Were I to go day by day and hour by hour over that time of trouble, the story would not please any one. Many were brave and forgot their own sorrows to occupy themselves with those of others, but many also were not brave. There were those among us who murmured and complained. Some would contend with us to let them go and call their husbands, and leave the miserable country where such things could happen. Some would rave against the priests and the government, and some against those who neglected and offended the Holy Church. Among them there were those who did not hesitate to say it was our fault, though how we were answerable they could not tell. We were never at any time of the day or night without a sound of some one weeping or bewailing herself, as if she were the only sufferer, or crying out against those who had brought her here, far from all her friends. By times it seemed to me that I could bear it no longer, that it was but justice to turn those murmurers *(pleureuses)* away, and let them try what better they could do for themselves. But in this point Madame Martin surpassed me. I do not grudge to say it. She was better than I was, for she was more patient. She wept with the weeping women, then dried her eyes and smiled upon them without a thought of anger—whereas I could have turned them to the door. One thing, however, which I could not away with, was that Agnès filled her own chamber with the poorest of the poor. 'How, ' I cried, thyself and thy friend Madame de Bois-Sombre, were you not enough to fill it, that you should throw open that chamber to good-for-nothings, to *va-nu-pieds*, to the very rabble? ' '*Ma mère,* ' said Madame Martin, 'our good Lord died for them. ' 'And surely for thee too, thou saint-imbécile! ' I cried out in my indignation. What, my Martin's chamber which he had adorned for his bride! I was beside myself. And they have an obstinacy these enthusiasts! But for that matter her friend Madame de Bois-Sombre thought the same. She would have been one of the *pleureuses* herself had it not been for shame. 'Agnès wishes to aid the *bon Dieu*, Madame, ' she said, 'to make us suffer still a little more. ' The tone in which she spoke, and the contraction in her forehead, as if our hospitality was not enough for her, turned my heart again to my daughter-in-law. 'You have reason, Madame, ' I cried; 'there are indeed many ways in which Agnès does the work of the good God. ' The Bois-Sombres are poor, they have not a roof to shelter them save that of the old hotel in Semur, from whence they were sent forth like the rest of us. And she and her children owed all to Agnès. Figure to yourself then my resentment when this lady directed her scorn at my daughter-in-law. I am not myself noble, though of the *haute bourgeoisie*, which some people think a purer race.

Long and terrible were the days we spent in this suspense. For ourselves it was well that there was so much to do—the food to provide for all this multitude, the little children to care for, and to prepare the provisions for our men who were before Semur. I was in the Ardennes during the war, and I saw some of its perils—but these were nothing to what we encountered now. It is true that my son Martin was not in the war, which made it very different to me; but here the dangers were such as we could not understand, and they weighed upon our spirits. The seat at the door, and that point where the road turned, where there was always so beautiful a view of the valley and of the town of Semur—were constantly occupied by groups of poor people gazing at the darkness in which their homes lay. It was strange to see them, some kneeling and praying with moving lips; some taking but one look, not able to endure the sight. I was of these last. From time to time, whenever I had a moment, I came out, I know not why, to see if there was any change. But to gaze upon that altered prospect for hours, as some did, would have been intolerable to me. I could not linger nor try to imagine what might be passing there, either among those who were within (as was believed), or those who were without the walls. Neither could I pray as many did. My devotions of every day I will never, I trust, forsake or forget, and that my Martin was always in my mind is it needful to say? But to go over and over all the vague fears that were in me, and all those thoughts which would have broken my heart had they been put into words, I could not do this even to the good Lord Himself. When I suffered myself to think, my heart grew sick, my head swam round, the light went from my eyes. They are happy who can do so, who can take the *bon Dieu* into their confidence, and say all to Him; but me, I could not do it. I could not dwell upon that which was so terrible, upon my home abandoned, my son—Ah! now that it is past, it is still terrible to think of. And then it was all I was capable of, to trust my God and do what was set before me. God, He knows what it is we can do and what we cannot. I could not tell even to Him all the terror and the misery and the darkness there was in me; but I put my faith in Him. It was all of which I was capable. We are not made alike, neither in the body nor in the soul.

And there were many women like me at La Clairière. When we had done each piece of work we would look out with a kind of hope, then go back to find something else to do—not looking at each other, not saying a word. Happily there was a great deal to do. And to see how some of the women, and those the most anxious, would work, never resting, going on from one thing to another, as if they were hungry for more and more! Some did it with their mouths shut close, with their countenances fixed, not daring to pause or meet another's eyes; but some, who were more patient, worked with a soft word, and sometimes a smile, and sometimes a tear; but ever working on. Some of them were an example to us all. In the morning, when we got up, some from beds, some from the floor, —I insisted that all should lie down, by turns at least, for we could not make room for every one at the same hours, —the very first thought of all was to hasten to the window, or, better, to the door. Who could tell what might have happened while we slept? For the first moment no one would speak, —it was the moment of hope—and then there would be a cry, a clasping of the hands, which told—what we all knew. The one of the women who touched my heart most was the wife of Riou of the *octroi*. She had been almost rich for her condition in life, with a good house and a little servant whom she trained admirably, as I have had occasion to know. Her husband and her son were both among those whom we had left under the walls of Semur; but she had three children with her at La Clairière. Madame Riou slept lightly, and so did I. Sometimes I heard her stir in the middle of the night, though so softly that no one woke. We were in the same room, for it may be supposed that to keep a room to one's self was not possible. I did not stir, but lay and watched her as she went to the window, her figure visible against the pale dawning of the light, with an eager quick movement as of expectation—then turning back with slower step and a sigh. She was always full of hope. As the days went on, there came to be a kind of communication between us. We understood each other. When one was occupied and the other free, that one of us who went out to the door to look across the valley where Semur was would look at the other as if to say, 'I go. ' When it was Madame Riou who did this, I shook my head, and she gave me a smile which awoke at every repetition (though I knew it was vain) a faint expectation, a little hope. When she came back, it was she who would shake her head, with her eyes full of tears. 'Did I not tell thee? ' I said, speaking to her as if she were my daughter. 'It will be for next time, Madame, ' she would say, and smile, yet put her apron to her eyes. There were many who were like her, and there were those of whom I have spoken who were *pleureuses*, never hoping anything, doing little, bewailing themselves and their hard fate. Some of them we employed to carry the provisions to Semur, and this amused them, though the heaviness of the baskets made again a complaint.

As for the children, thank God! they were not disturbed as we were—to them it was a beautiful holiday—it was like Heaven. There is no place on earth that I love like Semur, yet it is true that the streets are narrow, and there is not much room for the children. Here they were happy as the day; they strayed over all our gardens and the meadows, which were full of flowers; they sat in companies upon the green grass, as thick as the daisies themselves, which they loved. Old Sister Mariette, who is called Marie de la Consolation, sat out in the meadow under an acacia-tree and watched over them. She was the one among us who was happy. She had no son, no husband, among the watchers, and though, no doubt, she loved her convent and her hospital, yet she sat all day long in the shade and in the full air, and smiled, and never looked towards Semur. 'The good Lord will do as He wills, ' she said, 'and that will be well. ' It was true—we all knew it was true; but it might be—who could tell? —that it was His will to destroy our town, and take away our bread, and perhaps the lives of those who were dear to us; and something came in our throats which prevented a reply. '*Ma soeur,* ' I said, 'we are of the world, we tremble for those we love; we are not as you are. ' Sister Mariette did nothing but smile upon us. 'I have known my Lord these sixty years, ' she said, 'and He has taken everything from me. ' To see her smile as she said this was more than I could bear. From me He had taken something, but not all. Must we be prepared to give up all if we would be perfected? There were many of the others also who trembled at these words. 'And now He gives me my consolation, ' she said, and called the little ones round her, and told them a tale of the Good Shepherd, which is out of the holy Gospel. To see all the little ones round her knees in a crowd, and the peaceful face with which she smiled upon them, and the meadows all full of flowers, and the sunshine coming and going through the branches: and to hear that tale of Him who went forth to seek the lamb that was lost, was like a tale out of a holy book, where all was peace and goodness and joy. But on the other side, not twenty steps off, was the house full of those who wept, and at all the doors and windows anxious faces gazing down upon that cloud in the valley where Semur was. A procession of our women was coming back, many with lingering steps, carrying the baskets which were empty. 'Is there any news? ' we asked, reading their faces before they could answer. And some shook their heads, and some wept. There was no other reply.

On the last night before our deliverance, suddenly, in the middle of the night, there was a great commotion in the house. We all rose out of our beds at the sound of the cry, almost believing that some one at the window had seen the lifting of the cloud, and rushed together, frightened, yet all in an eager expectation to hear what it was. It was in the room where the old Mère Julie slept that the disturbance was. Mère Julie was one of the market-women of Semur, the one I have mentioned who was devout, who never missed the *Salut* in the afternoon, besides all masses which are obligatory. But there were other matters in which she had not satisfied my mind, as I have before said. She was the mother of Jacques Richard, who was a good-for-nothing, as is well known. At La Clairière Mère Julie had enacted a strange part. She had taken no part in anything that was done, but had established herself in the chamber allotted to her, and taken the best bed in it, where she kept her place night and day, making the others wait upon her. She had always expressed a great devotion for St. Jean; and the Sisters of the Hospital had been very kind to her, and also to her *vaurien* of a son, who was indeed, in some manner, the occasion of all our troubles—being the first who complained of the opening of the chapel into the chief ward, which was closed up by the administration, and thus became, as I and many others think, the cause of all the calamities that have come upon us. It was her bed that was the centre of the great commotion we had heard, and a dozen voices immediately began to explain to us as we entered. 'Mère Julie has had a dream. She has seen a vision, ' they said. It was a vision of angels in the most beautiful robes, all shining with gold and whiteness.

'The dress of the Holy Mother which she wears on the great *fêtes* was nothing to them, ' Mere Julie told us, when she had composed herself. For all had run here and there at her first cry, and procured for her a *tisane*, and a cup of *bouillon*, and all that was good for an attack of the nerves, which was what it was at first supposed to be. 'Their wings were like the wings of the great peacock on the terrace, but also like those of eagles. And each one had a collar of beautiful jewels about his neck, and robes whiter than those of any bride. ' This was the description she gave: and to see the women how they listened, head above head, a cloud of eager faces, all full of awe and attention! The angels had promised her that they would come again, when we had bound ourselves to observe all the functions of the Church, and when all these Messieurs had been converted, and made their submission—to lead us back gloriously to Semur. There was a great tumult in the chamber, and all cried out that they were convinced, that they were ready to promise. All except Madame Martin, who stood and looked at them with a look which surprised me, which was of pity rather than sympathy. As there was no one else to speak, I took the word, being the mother of the present Maire, and wife of the last, and in part mistress of the house. Had Agnès spoken I would have yielded to her, but as she was silent I took my right. 'Mère Julie, ' I said, 'and mes bonnes femmes, my friends, know you that it is the middle of the night, the hour at which we must rest if we are to be able to do the work that is needful, which the *bon Dieu* has laid upon us? It is not from us—my daughter and myself—who, it is well known, have followed all the functions of the Church, that you will meet with an opposition to your promise. But what I desire is that you should calm yourselves, that you should retire and rest till the time of work, husbanding your strength, since we know not what claim may be made upon it. The holy angels, ' I said, 'will comprehend, or if not they, then the *bon Dieu,* who understands everything. '

But it was with difficulty that I could induce them to listen to me, to do that which was reasonable. When, however, we had quieted the agitation, and persuaded the good women to repose themselves, it was no longer possible for me to rest. I promised to myself a little moment of quiet, for my heart longed to be alone. I stole out as quietly as I might, not to disturb any one, and sat down upon the bench outside the door. It was still a kind of half-dark, nothing visible, so that if any one should gaze and gaze down the valley, it was not possible to see what was there: and I was glad that it was not possible, for my very soul was tired. I sat down and leant my back upon the wall of our house, and opened my lips to draw in the air of the morning. How still it was! the very birds not yet begun to rustle and stir in the bushes; the night air hushed, and scarcely the first faint tint of blue beginning to steal into the darkness. When I had sat there a little, closing my eyes, lo, tears began to steal into them like rain when there has been a fever of heat. I have wept in my time many tears, but the time of weeping is over with me, and through all these miseries I had shed none. Now they came without asking, like a benediction refreshing my eyes. Just then I felt a soft pressure upon my shoulder, and there was Agnès coming close, putting her shoulder to mine, as was her way, that we might support each other.

'You weep, ma mère, ' she said.

'I think it is one of the angels Mère Julie has seen, ' said I. 'It is a refreshment—a blessing; my eyes were dry with weariness. '

'Mother, ' said Madame Martin, 'do you think it is angels with wings like peacocks and jewelled collars that our Father sends to us? Ah, not so—one of those whom we love has touched your dear eyes, ' and with that she kissed me upon my eyes, taking me in her arms. My heart is sometimes hard to my son's wife, but not always—not with my will, God knows! Her kiss was soft as the touch of any angel could be.

'God bless thee, my child, ' I said.

'Thanks, thanks, ma mère! ' she cried. 'Now I am resolved; now will I go and speak to Martin—of something in my heart. '

'What will you do, my child? ' I said, for as the light increased I could see the meaning in her face, and that it was wrought up for some great thing. 'Beware, Agnès; risk not my son's happiness by risking thyself; thou art more to Martin than all the world beside. '

'He loves thee dearly, mother, ' she said. My heart was comforted. I was able to remember that I too had had my day. 'He loves his mother, thank God, but not as he loves thee. Beware, *ma fille*. If you risk my son's happiness, neither will I forgive you. ' She smiled upon me, and kissed my hands.

'I will go and take him his food and some linen, and carry him your love and mine. '

'*You* will go, and carry one of those heavy baskets with the others! '

'Mother, ' cried Agnès, 'now you shame me that I have never done it before. '

What could I say? Those whose turn it was were preparing their burdens to set out. She had her little packet made up, besides, of our cool white linen, which I knew would be so grateful to my son. I went with her to the turn of the road, helping her with her basket; but my limbs trembled, what with the long continuance of the trial, what with the agitation of the night. It was but just daylight when they went away, disappearing down the long slope of the road that led to Semur. I went back to the bench at the door, and there I sat down and thought. Assuredly it was wrong to close up the chapel, to deprive the sick of the benefit of the holy mass. But yet I could not but reflect that the *bon Dieu* had suffered still more great scandals to take place without such a punishment. When, however, I reflected on all that has been done by those who have no cares of this world as we have, but are brides of Christ, and upon all they resign by their dedication, and the claim they have to be furthered, not hindered, in their holy work: and when I bethought myself how many and great are the powers of evil, and that, save in us poor women who can do so little, the Church has few friends: then it came back to me how heinous was the offence that had been committed, and that it might well be that the saints out of heaven should return to earth to take the part and avenge the cause of the weak. My husband would have been the first to do it, had he seen with my eyes; but though in the flesh he did not do so, is it to be doubted that in heaven their eyes are enlightened—those who have been subjected to the cleansing fires and have ascended into final bliss? This all became clear to me as I sat and pondered, while the morning light grew around me, and the sun rose and shed his first rays, which are as precious gold, on the summits of the mountains—for at La Clairière we are nearer the mountains than at Semur.

The house was more still than usual, and all slept to a later hour because of the agitation of the past night. I had been seated, like old sister Mariette, with my eyes turned rather towards the hills than to the valley, being so deep in my thoughts that I did not look, as it was our constant wont to look, if any change had happened over Semur. Thus blessings come unawares when we are not looking for them. Suddenly I lifted my eyes—but not with expectation—languidly, as one looks without thought. Then it was that I gave that great cry which brought all crowding to the windows, to the gardens, to every spot from whence that blessed sight was visible; for there before us, piercing through the clouds, were the beautiful towers of Semur, the Cathedral with all its pinnacles, that are as if they were carved out of foam, and the solid tower of St. Lambert, and the others, every one. They told me after that I flew, though I am past running, to the farmyard to call all the labourers and servants of the farm, bidding them prepare every carriage and waggon, and even the *charrettes*, to carry back the children, and those who could not walk to the city.

'The men will be wild with privation and trouble, ' I said to myself; 'they will want the sight of their little children, the comfort of their wives. '

I did not wait to reason nor to ask myself if I did well; and my son has told me since that he scarcely was more thankful for our great deliverance than, just when the crowd of gaunt and weary men returned into Semur, and there was a moment when excitement and joy were at their highest, and danger possible, to hear the roll of the heavy farm waggons, and to see me arrive, with all the little ones and their mothers, like a new army, to take possession of their homes once more.

M. LE MAIRE CONCLUDES HIS RECORD.

The narratives which I have collected from the different eye-witnesses during the time of my own absence, will show how everything passed while I, with M. le Curé, was recovering possession of our city. Many have reported to me verbally the occurrences of the last half-hour before my return; and in their accounts there are naturally discrepancies, owing to their different points of view and different ways of regarding the subject. But all are agreed that a strange and universal slumber had seized upon all. M. de Bois-Sombre even admits that he, too, was overcome by this influence. They slept while we were performing our dangerous and solemn duty in Semur. But when the Cathedral bells began to ring, with one impulse all awoke; and starting from the places where they lay, from the shade of the trees and bushes and sheltering hollows, saw the cloud and the mist and the darkness which had enveloped Semur suddenly rise from the walls. It floated up into the higher air before their eyes, then was caught and carried away, and flung about into shreds upon the sky by a strong wind, of which down below no influence was felt. They all gazed, not able to get their breath, speechless, beside themselves with joy, and saw the walls reappear, and the roofs of the houses, and our glorious Cathedral against the blue sky. They stood for a moment spell-bound. M. de Bois-Sombre informs me that he was afraid of a wild rush into the city, and himself hastened to the front to lead and restrain it; when suddenly a great cry rang through the air, and some one was seen to fall across the high road, straight in front of the Porte St. Lambert. M. de Bois-Sombre was at once aware who it was, for he himself had watched Lecamus taking his place at the feet of my wife, who awaited my return there. This checked the people in their first rush towards their homes; and when it was seen that Madame Dupin had also sunk down fainting on the ground after her more than human exertions for the comfort of all, there was but one impulse of tenderness and pity. When I reached the gate on my return, I found my wife lying there in all the pallor of death, and for a moment my heart stood still with sudden terror. What mattered Semur to me, if it had cost me my Agnès? or how could I think of Lecamus or any other, while she lay between life and death? I had her carried back to our own house. She was the first to re-enter Semur; and after a time, thanks be to God, she came back to herself. But Paul Lecamus was a dead man. No need to carry him in, to attempt unavailing cares. 'He has gone, that one; he has marched with the others, ' said the old doctor, who had served in his day, and sometimes would use the language of the camp. He cast but one glance at him, and laid his hand upon his heart in passing. 'Cover his face, ' was all he said.

It is possible that this check was good for the restraint of the crowd. It moderated the rush with which they returned to their homes. The sight of the motionless figures stretched out by the side of the way overawed them. Perhaps it may seem strange, to any one who has known what had occurred, that the state of the city should have given me great anxiety the first night of our return. The withdrawal of the oppression and awe which had been on the men, the return of everything to its natural state, the sight of their houses unchanged, so that the brain turned round of these common people, who seldom reflect upon anything, and they already began to ask themselves was it all a delusion—added to the exhaustion of their physical condition, and the natural desire for ease and pleasure after the long strain upon all their faculties—produced an excitement which might have led to very disastrous consequences. Fortunately I had foreseen this. I have always been considered to possess great knowledge of human nature, and this has been matured by recent events. I sent off messengers instantly to bring home the women and children, and called around me the men in whom I could most trust. Though I need not say that the excitement and suffering of the past three days had told not less upon myself than upon others, I abandoned all idea of rest. The first thing that I did, aided by my respectable fellow-townsmen, was to take possession of all *cabarets* and wine-shops, allowing indeed the proprietors to return, but preventing all assemblages within them. We then established a patrol of respectable citizens throughout the city, to preserve the public peace. I calculated, with great anxiety, how many hours it would be before my messengers could react: La Clairière, to bring back the women—for in such a case the wives are the best guardians, and can exercise an influence more general and less suspected than that of the magistrates; but this was not to be hoped for for three or four hours at least. Judge, then, what was my joy and satisfaction when the sound of wheels (in itself a pleasant sound, for no wheels had been audible on the high-road since these events began) came briskly to us from the distance; and looking out from the watch-tower over the Porte St. Lambert, I saw the strangest procession. The wine-carts and all the farm vehicles of La Clairière, and every kind of country waggon, were jolting along the road, all in a tumult and babble of delicious voices; and from under the rude canopies and awnings and roofs of vine branches, made up to shield them from the sun, lo!

there were the children like birds in a nest, one little head peeping over the other. And the cries and songs, the laughter, and the shoutings! As they came along the air grew sweet, the world was made new. Many of us, who had borne all the terrors and sufferings of the past without fainting, now felt their strength fail them. Some broke out into tears, interrupted with laughter. Some called out aloud the names of their little ones. We went out to meet them, every man there present, myself at the head. And I will not deny that a sensation of pride came over me when I saw my mother stand up in the first waggon, with all those happy ones fluttering around her. 'My son, ' she said, 'I have discharged the trust that was given me. I bring thee back the blessing of God. ' 'And God bless thee, my mother! ' I cried. The other men, who were fathers, like me, came round me, crowding to kiss her hand. It is not among the women of my family that you will find those who abandon their duties.

And then to lift them down in armfuls, those flowers of paradise, all fresh with the air of the fields, all joyous like the birds! We put them down by twos and threes, some of us sobbing with joy. And to see them dispersing hand in hand, running here and there, each to its home, carrying peace, and love, and gladness, through the streets—that was enough to make the most serious smile. No fear was in them, or care. Every haggard man they met—some of them feverish, restless, beginning to think of riot and pleasure after forced abstinence—there was a new shout, a rush of little feet, a shower of soft kisses. The women were following after, some packed into the carts and waggons, pale and worn, yet happy; some walking behind in groups; the more strong, or the more eager, in advance, and a long line of stragglers behind. There was anxiety in their faces, mingled with their joy. How did they know what they might find in the houses from which they had been shut out? And many felt, like me, that in the very return, in the relief, there was danger. But the children feared nothing; they filled the streets with their dear voices, and happiness came back with them. When I felt my little Jean's cheek against mine, then for the first time did I know how much anguish I had suffered—how terrible was parting, and how sweet was life. But strength and prudence melt away when one indulges one's self, even in one's dearest affections. I had to call my guardians together, to put mastery upon myself, that a just vigilance might not be relaxed. M. de Bois-Sombre, though less anxious than myself, and disposed to believe (being a soldier) that a little license would do no harm, yet stood by me; and, thanks to our precautions, all went well.

Before night three parts of the population had returned to Semur, and the houses were all lighted up as for a great festival. The Cathedral stood open—even the great west doors, which are only opened on great occasions—with a glow of tapers gleaming out on every side. As I stood in the twilight watching, and glad at heart to think that all was going well, my mother and my wife—still pale, but now recovered from her fainting and weakness—came out into the great square, leading my little Jean. They were on their way to the Cathedral, to thank God for their return. They looked at me, but did not ask me to go with them, those dear women; they respected my opinions, as I had always respected theirs. But this silence moved me more than words; there came into my heart a sudden inspiration. I was still in my scarf of office, which had been, I say it without vanity, the standard of authority and protection during all our trouble; and thus marked out as representative of all, I uncovered myself, after the ladies of my family had passed, and, without joining them, silently followed with a slow and solemn step. A suggestion, a look, is enough for my countrymen; those who were in the Place with me perceived in a moment what I meant. One by one they uncovered, they put themselves behind me. Thus we made such a procession as had never been seen in Semur. We were gaunt and worn with watching and anxiety, which only added to the solemn effect. Those who were already in the Cathedral, and especially M. le Curé, informed me afterwards that the tramp of our male feet as we came up the great steps gave to all a thrill of expectation and awe. It was at the moment of the exposition of the Sacrament that we entered. Instinctively, in a moment, all understood—a thing which could happen nowhere but in France, where intelligence is swift as the breath on our lips. Those who were already there yielded their places to us, most of the women rising up, making as it were a ring round us, the tears running down their faces. When the Sacrament was replaced upon the altar, M. le Curé, perceiving our meaning, began at once in his noble voice to intone the *Te Deum*. Rejecting all other music, he adopted the plain song in which all could join, and with one voice, every man in unison with his brother, we sang with him. The great Cathedral walls seemed to throb with the sound that rolled upward, *mâle* and deep, as no song has ever risen from Semur in the memory of man. The women stood up around us, and wept and sobbed with pride and joy. When this wonderful moment was over, and all the people poured forth out of the Cathedral walls into the soft evening, with stars shining above, and all the friendly lights below, there was such a tumult of emotion and gladness as I have never seen before. Many of the poor women surrounded me, kissed my hand notwithstanding my resistance, and called upon God to bless me; while some of the older persons made remarks full of justice and feeling.

'The *bon Dieu* is not used to such singing, ' one of them cried, her old eyes streaming with tears. 'It must have surprised the saints up in heaven! '

'It will bring a blessing, ' cried another. 'It is not like our little voices, that perhaps only reach half-way. '

This was figurative language, yet it was impossible to doubt there was much truth in it. Such a submission of our intellects, as I felt in determining to make it, must have been pleasing to heaven. The women, they are always praying; but when we thus presented ourselves to give thanks, it meant something, a real homage; and with a feeling of solemnity we separated, aware that we had contented both earth and heaven.

Next morning there was a great function in the Cathedral, at which the whole city assisted. Those who could not get admittance crowded upon the steps, and knelt half way across the Place. It was an occasion long remembered in Semur, though I have heard many say not in itself so impressive as the *Te Deum* on the evening of our return. After this we returned to our occupations, and life was resumed under its former conditions in our city.

It might be supposed, however, that the place in which events so extraordinary had happened would never again be as it was before. Had I not been myself so closely involved, it would have appeared to me certain, that the streets, trod once by such inhabitants as those who for three nights and days abode within Semur, would have always retained some trace of their presence; that life there would have been more solemn than in other places; and that those families for whose advantage the dead had risen out of their graves, would have henceforward carried about with them some sign of that interposition. It will seem almost incredible when I now add that nothing of this kind has happened at Semur. The wonderful manifestation which interrupted our existence has passed absolutely as if it had never been. We had not been twelve hours in our houses ere we had forgotten, or practically forgotten, our expulsion from them. Even myself, to whom everything was so vividly brought home, I have to enter my wife's room to put aside the curtain from little Marie's picture, and to see and touch the olive branch which is there, before I can recall to myself anything that resembles the feeling with which I re-entered that sanctuary. My grandfather's bureau still stands in the middle of my library, where I found it on my return; but I have got used to it, and it no longer affects me. Everything is as it was; and I cannot persuade myself that, for a time, I and mine were shut out, and our places taken by those who neither eat nor drink, and whose life is invisible to our eyes. Everything, I say, is as it was—every thing goes on as if it would endure for ever. We know this cannot be, yet it does not move us. Why, then, should the other move us? A little time, we are aware, and we, too, shall be as they are—as shadows, and unseen. But neither has the one changed us, and neither does the other. There was, for some time, a greater respect shown to religion in Semur, and a more devout attendance at the sacred functions; but I regret to say this did not continue. Even in my own case—I say it with sorrow—it did not continue. M. le Curé is an admirable person. I know no more excellent ecclesiastic. He is indefatigable in the performance of his spiritual duties; and he has, besides, a noble and upright soul. Since the days when we suffered and laboured together, he has been to me as a brother. Still, it is undeniable that he makes calls upon our credulity, which a man obeys with reluctance. There are ways of surmounting this; as I see in Agnès for one, and in M. de Bois-Sombre for another. My wife does not question, she believes much; and in respect to that which she cannot acquiesce in, she is silent. 'There are many things I hear you talk of, Martin, which are strange to me, ' she says, 'of myself I cannot believe in them; but I do not oppose, since it is possible you may have reason to know better than I; and so with some things that we hear from M. le Curé. ' This is how she explains herself—but she is a woman. It is a matter of grace to yield to our better judgment. M. de Bois-Sombre has another way. '*Ma foi,* ' he says, 'I have not the time for all your delicacies, my good people; I have come to see that these things are for the advantage of the world, and it is not my business to explain them. If M. le Curé attempted to criticise me in military matters, or thee, my excellent Martin, in affairs of business, or in the culture of your vines, I should think him not a wise man; and in like manner, faith and religion, these are his concern. ' Felix de Bois Sombre is an excellent fellow; but he smells a little of the *mousquetaire*. I, who am neither a soldier nor a woman, I have hesitations. Nevertheless, so long as I am Maire of Semur, nothing less than the most absolute respect shall ever be shown to all truly religious persons, with whom it is my earnest desire to remain in sympathy and fraternity, so far as that may be.

It seemed, however, a little while ago as if my tenure of this office would not be long, notwithstanding the services which I am acknowledged, on every hand, to have done to my fellow-townsmen. It will be remembered that when M. le Curé and myself found Semur empty, we heard a voice of complaining from the hospital of St. Jean, and found a sick man who had been left there, and who grumbled against the Sisters, and accused them of neglecting him, but remained altogether unaware, in the meantime, of what had happened in the city. Will it be believed that after a time this fellow was put faith in as a seer, who had heard and beheld many things of which we were all ignorant? It must be said that, in the meantime, there had been a little excitement in the town on the subject of the chapel in the hospital, to which repeated reference has already been made. It was insisted on behalf of these ladies that a promise had been given, taking, indeed, the form of a vow, that, as soon as we were again in possession of Semur, their full privileges should be restored to them. Their advocates even went so far as to send to me a deputation of those who had been nursed in the hospital, the leader of which was Jacques Richard, who since he has been, as he says, 'converted, ' thrusts himself to the front of every movement.

'Permit me to speak, M. le Maire, ' he said; 'me, who was one of those so misguided as to complain, before the great lesson we have all received. The mass did not disturb any sick person who was of right dispositions. I was then a very bad subject, indeed—as, alas! M. le Maire too well knows. It annoyed me only as all pious observances annoyed me. I am now, thank heaven, of a very different way of thinking— —'

But I would not listen to the fellow. When he was a *mauvais sujet* he was less abhorrent to me than now.

The men were aware that when I pronounced myself so distinctly on any subject, there was nothing more to be said, for, though gentle as a lamb and open to all reasonable arguments, I am capable of making the most obstinate stand for principle; and to yield to popular superstition, is that worthy of a man who has been instructed? At the same time it raised a great anger in my mind that all that should be thought of was a thing so trivial. That they should have given themselves, soul and body, for a little money; that they should have scoffed at all that was noble and generous, both in religion and in earthly things; all that was nothing to them. And now they would insult the great God Himself by believing that all He cared for was a little mass in a convent chapel. What desecration! What debasement! When I went to M. le Curé, he smiled at my vehemence. There was pain in his smile, and it might be indignation; but he was not furious like me.

'They will conquer you, my friend, ' he said.

'Never, ' I cried. 'Before I might have yielded. But to tell me the gates of death have been rolled back, and Heaven revealed, and the great God stooped down from Heaven, in order that mass should be said according to the wishes of the community in the midst of the sick wards! They will never make me believe this, if I were to die for it. '

'Nevertheless, they will conquer, ' M. le Curé said.

It angered me that he should say so. My heart was sore as if my friend had forsaken me. And then it was that the worst step was taken in this crusade of false religion. It was from my mother that I heard of it first. One day she came home in great excitement, saying that now indeed a real light was to be shed upon all that had happened to us.

'It appears, ' she said, 'that Pierre Plastron was in the hospital all the time, and heard and saw many wonderful things. Sister Genevieve has just told me. It is wonderful beyond anything you could believe. He has spoken with our holy patron himself, St. Lambert, and has received instructions for a pilgrimage—'

'Pierre Plastron! ' I cried; 'Pierre Plastron saw nothing, ma mère. He was not even aware that anything remarkable had occurred. He complained to us of the Sisters that they neglected him; he knew nothing more. '

'My son, ' she said, looking upon me with reproving eyes, 'what have the good Sisters done to thee? Why is it that you look so unfavourably upon everything that comes from the community of St. Jean? '

'What have I to do with the community? ' I cried—'when I tell thee, Maman, that this Pierre Plastron knows nothing! I heard it from the fellow's own lips, and M. le Curé was present and heard him too. He had seen nothing, he knew nothing. Inquire of M. le Curé, if you have doubts of me. '

'I do not doubt you, Martin, ' said my mother, with severity, 'when you are not biassed by prejudice. And, as for M. le Curé, it is well known that the clergy are often jealous of the good Sisters, when they are not under their own control. '

Such was the injustice with which we were treated. And next day nothing was talked of but the revelation of Pierre Plastron. What he had seen and what he had heard was wonderful. All the saints had come and talked with him, and told him what he was to say to his townsmen. They told him exactly how everything had happened: how St. Jean himself had interfered on behalf of the Sisters, and how, if we were not more attentive to the duties of religion, certain among us would be bound hand and foot and cast into the jaws of hell. That I was one, nay the chief, of these denounced persons, no one could have any doubt. This exasperated me; and as soon as I knew that this folly had been printed and was in every house, I hastened to M. le Curé, and entreated him in his next Sunday's sermon to tell the true story of Pierre Plastron, and reveal the imposture. But M. le Curé shook his head. 'It will do no good, ' he said.

'But how no good? ' said I. 'What good are we looking for? These are lies, nothing but lies. Either he has deceived the poor ladies basely, or they themselves—but this is what I cannot believe. '

'Dear friend, ' he said, 'compose thyself. Have you never discovered yet how strong is self-delusion? There will be no lying of which they are aware. Figure to yourself what a stimulus to the imagination to know that he was here, actually here. Even I—it suggests a hundred things to me. The Sisters will have said to him (meaning no evil, nay meaning the edification of the people), "But, Pierre, reflect! You must have seen this and that. Recall thy recollections a little. " And by degrees Pierre will have found out that he remembered—more than could have been hoped. '

'*Mon Dieu*! ' I cried, out of patience, 'and you know all this, yet you will not tell them the truth—the very truth. '

'To what good? ' he said. Perhaps M. le Curé was right: but, for my part, had I stood up in that pulpit, I should have contradicted their lies and given no quarter. This, indeed, was what I did both in my private and public capacity; but the people, though they loved me, did not believe me. They said, 'The best men have their prejudices. M. le Maire is an excellent man; but what will you? He is but human after all. '

M. le Curé and I said no more to each other on this subject. He was a brave man, yet here perhaps he was not quite brave. And the effect of Pierre Plastron's revelations in other quarters was to turn the awe that had been in many minds into mockery and laughter. '*Ma foi,* ' said Félix de Bois-Sombre, 'Monseigneur St. Lambert has bad taste, mon ami Martin, to choose Pierre Plastron for his confidant when he might have had thee. ' 'M. de Bois-Sombre does ill to laugh, ' said my mother (even my mother! she was not on my side), 'when it is known that the foolish are often chosen to confound the wise. ' But Agnès, my wife, it was she who gave me the best consolation. She turned to me with the tears in her beautiful eyes.

'Mon ami, ' she said, 'let Monseigneur St. Lambert say what he will. He is not God that we should put him above all. There were other saints with other thoughts that came for thee and for me! '

All this contradiction was over when Agnès and I together took our flowers on the *jour des morts* to the graves we love. Glimmering among the rest was a new cross which I had not seen before. This was the inscription upon it: —

À PAUL LECAMUS
PARTI
LE 20 JUILLET, 1875
AVEC LES BIEN-AIMÉS

On it was wrought in the marble a little branch of olive. I turned to look at my wife as she laid underneath this cross a handful of violets. She gave me her hand still fragrant with the flowers. There was none of his family left to put up for him any token of human remembrance. Who but she should have done it, who had helped him to join that company and army of the beloved? 'This was our brother, ' she said; 'he will tell my Marie what use I made of her olive leaves. '

THE END

CPSIA information can be obtained at www.ICGtesting.com
Printed in the USA
LVOW10s1715231215

467601LV00001B/47/P